EARTHBOUND

Also by Richard Matheson

RICHARD MATHESON

EARTHBOUND

TOR

A Tom Doherty Associates Book
New York

For Ruth Ann

Thou art my own, my darling and my wife
And when we pass into another life
Still thou art mine

—*A. J. Munby*,
Marriage

EARTHBOUND

First published in the United Kingdom by Robinson Publishing in 1989. First published in substantially different form in the United States under the pseudonym Logan Swanson in 1982.

This book is printed on acid-free paper.

A Tor® Book
Published by Tom Doherty Associates, Inc.
175 Fifth Avenue
New York, N.Y. 10010

Tor® is a registered trademark of Tom Doherty Associates, Inc.

ISBN 0-312-85712-8

First edition: August 1994

Printed in the United States of America

0 9 8 7 6 5 4 3 2 1

THURSDAY

They reached the cottage a little after four that afternoon. David parked the car in front of it and he and Ellen sat in silence, looking at its faded clapboard siding, its torn, rusty screens and grime-streaked windows. Finally, David said, "I wonder if Roderick and Madeline are expecting us."

Ellen responded with a faint noise but whether of amusement or distress—or both—David couldn't tell. He turned to her and smiled consolingly. "You want to try some other place?" he asked.

She faced him in surprise. "But the realtor told us there was no other place," she said.

"Not here, no."

Her expression deepened. "Not in Logan Beach?"

"I mean—" David gestured aimlessly "—rather than stay where it's unpleasant for you." He managed another smile. "It would only be for the nights," he said. "We'd spend the days here."

Ellen nodded vaguely, looking at the cottage again. They couldn't really spend the days here, David knew; if nothing else, it was too cold. Slumping back, he dropped his hands from the steering wheel and turned toward the muffled pounding of the surf. Odd that this place had survived when the other hadn't; it was just as close to the water.

"A pity the other cottage was destroyed," he said.

She answered quietly. "It *is* a pity."

David looked at her, trying to appraise her expression. There was sorrow in it, certainly; disappointment. Was there, also, resignation? Reaching out, he squeezed her hands where they lay, held together, on her lap.

"I'm not trying to change the plan," he said. "It's just that . . . well, we've come a long way. It would be a shame to stay in a place that depressed us."

She looked over worriedly. "Where would we go?" she asked.

"Oh—" He shrugged. "I'm sure there are places all along the Sound. We could—"

He stopped as Ellen shook her head determinedly. "No," she said. "I'm sure this one's all right. We haven't even checked inside and, already, we're condemning it." She smiled. "Come on, let's take a look."

"You're sure?"

"I'm sure." Ellen opened the door on her side and got out.

David pushed out the door and stood, wincing at the cramped stiffness of his legs. He stretched, then shivered as the icy wind bit through his jacket.

As they neared the back of the cottage, David noticed a bank of high windows on its second story. "That must be the studio," he said.

Ellen glanced up at the heavily draped windows.

"Must be quite a view from there," David said. He shivered fitfully. "Wow, it's cold!"

"I know."

Something in her tone—defeat, despondence—

made him look at her inquiringly. She noticed and forced a smile. "Don't mind me," she said. "A little terminal nostalgia, that's all." She looked around, attempting optimism. "Logan Beach hasn't changed that much."

"Except for our honeymoon haven being blown out to sea by a hurricane."

"That *is* a disappointment," Ellen said. "I'd looked forward to seeing it again."

"Maybe it's just as well," he said. He didn't look at her but, from the corners of his eyes, noted her questioning glance. "I mean—"

"What if it looked—different?" she supplied.

He nodded. "It's best that we always recall it as it was"—in 1960, his mind appended; dear God, *twenty-one years ago.* The thrust of pain was sudden, unanticipated. Momentarily, his veneer of pretense seemed to fall away. With dogged will, he forced it back. Taking the realtor's key from his jacket pocket, he slid it into the front door lock. The bottom of the door rubbed across frayed carpeting as he pushed it open.

"Shall I carry you across the threshold?"

"*Can* you?" She repressed a smile.

He glared at her in mock reproach. "The gall," he said, "and me a two-hour-a-week weight lifter." Bending over, he pressed his left arm behind her knees, his right against her lower back. "Allez-oop," he said.

"No; honey." Ellen's smile grew, suddenly, awkward. I was only teasing." She pulled away from him. "You'll hurt your back."

David straightened up.

"You don't want to spend your second honeymoon in bed, do you?" she asked.

"That is exactly where I want to spend it."

"A hospital bed?"

"Touché," he said.

As they entered, David grimaced. "If possible," he said, "it's colder inside than out."

Ellen smiled. "I'm sure a nice, big blaze in that fireplace would take the chill off."

David nodded as he glanced around. "It's not too bad," he said. When Ellen didn't respond, he looked at her. "Is it?"

"No, it's nice," she answered, without conviction.

He slipped an arm around her waist. "Come on," he said. "We'll find another place." Ellen looked at him, confusedly. "You don't like it here," he told her.

"Yes, I do."

"No, you don't. Come on, we'll look for—"

"No." She cut him off with such intensity that David was startled. "I mean—" She smiled self-consciously. "—We planned to spend the week at Logan Beach. It wouldn't be the same if we didn't."

"I know, but—"

"I like it, David; really. It's just the cold that—*there.*" She pointed. "There's the gas heater the realtor mentioned. We get that going in addition to the fireplace and it'll be as cozy as—" She gestured undecidedly.

"Christmas at the morgue?" he said.

She made a reproving face and moved into the living room. David watched her for a few moments, then turned and shut the door, shivering. The air seemed to possess almost a tangible mass, he thought; he envisioned it seeping into his lungs like some sub-zero liquid. Clenching his teeth as though to set a barrier against it, he followed Ellen into the dim-lit, shadowy room.

The raised-hearth, stone fireplace was to his left, centered on the west wall. Above the cobbled slab of its mantelpiece hung a painting of a sailboat yawing sharply in a turbulent sea. David squinted; it was an original in oils. He passed his gaze across the built-in bookcases on either side of the fireplace, the small, shade-covered windows above them. He looked at the furniture: the bulky sofa facing the fireplace, the arm-chairs, tables and lamps. They reminded him of furniture he'd seen illustrated in a 1937 Sears-Roebuck catalog borrowed from the research department of MGM.

"It isn't bad at all," Ellen said.

David glanced at her. "You really think so?"

She smiled at him. "I like it."

"All right," he said.

"Good, it's settled then. Let's look at the rest."

Something in her voice—a vestige of the eager, childlike quality he'd always loved—made him smile and put his arm around her. "Lead the way, Ellen Audrey," he said.

They moved across the faded carpeting, by-passed the narrow, wall-flanked staircase and moved into the dining alcove, the ceiling of which was only a few inches higher than the top of David's head. The niche-like room had a double window, nicely curtained; parquet flooring with a multicolored oval rug covering most of it; a circular maple table with four captain's chairs around it; a tarnished, copper light fixture suspended overhead; and, to the right of the kitchen door, a sideboard with a dust-filmed mirror hanging on the wall above it.

"This is kind of nice," Ellen said.

"Mmm-hmm."

David pushed open the swinging door and followed Ellen into the kitchen.

"Oh, well, it's nice and warm in here," he said, looking at the steam which clouded from his lips.

"Open the door and let the cold out," she suggested.

"Here's the trouble," David told her, crossing to the small refrigerator and pushing its door shut. He saw the wire and plug coiled on top of it. "Drat," he said. "And, here, I wanted some ice cubes."

"You can use my toes and fingers," Ellen said.

Smiling, David twisted one of the stove knobs without effect. He turned it back into place and looked around at the sink and counters, the windows, above them, facing the Sound; the windowed, shade-drawn door; the yellow, wooden table-and-chair set in the center of the worn, linoleum-covered floor. "Let's face it," he said, "it's the kitchen."

"Or the freezer," Ellen answered, turning with a shudder and returning to the dining alcove.

He found that he couldn't move, a weight of enervation holding him immobile. They should never have come back to Logan Beach; it had been a vain fancy on his part. He wished that they were in Sherman Oaks, in their comfortable hillside home. It seemed absurd that Mark should be alone there, with them a continent away.

"Honey?"

Ellen had pushed the swinging door half open and was looking at him curiously. "Something wrong?" she asked.

"No, no I'm just—" he forced a smile and started toward her "—daydreaming." *He mustn't ruin this for Ellen.* "Hey, we haven't looked upstairs yet."

Ellen returned his smile. "Let's take a look," she said.

They crossed the dining alcove and made a right turn onto the shadowy staircase, Ellen going first. As they started up the threadbare, carpeted steps, David looked at the assortment of small paintings hung along the stairwell, each of them a local coastal scene or seascape. "These must have been done by the same artist who did that painting over the fireplace," he said. He stopped to examine one which depicted the beach around the cottage. He pointed at the upper left-hand corner of it. "There's that mansion," he said.

Ellen stopped and looked around. "What a view they must have, way up on the bluff like that," she said.

"I wonder if the same people still live there," David said. "Not that we'd know if we saw them."

Halfway to the second floor was a landing with a door on its right. David twisted the icy, brass knob and stepped inside the darkened room. "God," he muttered. Ellen hissed and stopped beside him.

"This one is the worst of all," she said.

David crossed the wooden floor, his footsteps sounding thinly hollow. Drawing back an edge of drape, he looked out. "Quite a view," he said, impressed. "You can see—" He broke off as, in glancing back, he saw that Ellen was still by the doorway, arms crossed, teeth on edge. "Too cold?" he asked. She nodded jerkily.

The doughnut-sized curtain rings slid hissingly along their rod as David tugged the drape back, uncovering more than four feet of window. He looked around the huge room. It was empty except for a wooden work table standing near the east wall, its surface crosshatched with palette knife scars and spangled by paint spots, plus a sagging couch pushed against the wall by which he stood; David glanced at the faded pine cone and needle design on its slipcover, the folded blanket at its foot. "I doubt if we'll get much use from this room," he said.

Ellen didn't answer and he looked around. She was waiting for him on the staircase landing. Walking back, he left the studio and pulled the door almost shut. He put an arm around her shoulders as they started up the stairs again and Ellen shuddered. "You *are* cold," David said.

"It caught up with me."

They reached the second story landing and David opened the door in front of them, twitching at the shadowy image of himself and Ellen in the bathroom cabinet mirror. "There they are, folks," he said, "that frolicsome duo—Gooseflesh and Shivers." Ellen grunted, smiling wanly as he steered her to the left and opened the bedroom door. "Here we go," he said.

Leading Ellen across the dimlit bedroom, he sat her on the uncovered mattress of the maple four-poster. A checkered black and orange comforter was hung across the foot rail and he slid it off, coughing at the dust as he shook it open. "House is, obviously, in constant use," he said. He lay the comforter on Ellen's shoulders and tucked it around her body and underneath her legs. "There." Leaning over, he kissed the tip of her nose. "Like kissing a snowman," he said. He patted her shoulder and looked around. "Hey," he said, "just what you've always dreamed about—a fireplace in the bedroom."

"Put me in and light me," Ellen said, huddling, cringed, beneath the comforter.

David walked across the room and peered into the fireplace. "I do believe—" he said. He moved to the nearest window and raised its shade, returning to the fireplace to look inside again. "Yeah." He set aside the screen and, picking up a brown-edged newspaper from the raised hearth, crumpled several of its pages and stuffed them underneath the block of charred driftwood. There was an old book of matches on the mantel and lighting one, he held the flame against the paper which ignited instantly. He straightened from the flaring blaze and put the screen in place, then turned. "How does it look?" he asked.

"Like heaven," Ellen said.

Smiling, David moved back across the room and raised the shade of the dormer window. Looking down, he saw the car, the sight of it, suddenly, making him wish that they were in it, speeding back toward JFK where they could leave it at the rental agency and book passage on the first available flight to Los Angeles. He fought away the impulse, turned. Ellen was standing in front of the fireplace, the comforter held around her. David walked over and put an arm across her shoulders. "Better now?" he asked.

"Mm-hmm."

"Good."

They gazed into the crackling flames a while before David spoke. "It's going to work out fine, El," he told her.

She smiled but it was not convincing to him. He patted her back. "I'll get the luggage," he said.

"Want some help?"

"No, no, I can manage. Concentrate on getting warm."

She smiled. "All right."

David left the bedroom with the feeling of a prisoner in flight.

The wind had nearly stopped now. It was as cold as ever but, without the cleaving wind, in no way as unpleasant as it had been that afternoon. David felt almost comfortable as he drew up the lid of the woodbox behind the house. He started reaching in, then drew back his hand and peered inside. Wouldn't do to die of a spider bite on our second honeymoon, he thought. Seeing nothing, he reached down into the box and hauled out several sawed-up lengths of driftwood.

Closing the kitchen door by leaning back against it, he crossed the dark room, shouldered open the swinging door and moved through the alcove to the living room. Ellen was burning empty cracker boxes in the fireplace. Like him, she was dressed in bulky camping clothes.

"Sure you had enough to eat?" she asked as he dumped the wood on the hearth.

"Plenty." David removed his jacket and tossed one of the driftwood sections on the fire, jabbing it into place with the poker. He left the screen off and they sat beside each other on the sofa, propping their feet on the hearth. He put his arm around Ellen's shoulders and she leaned against him.

It had been a pleasant evening. Originally, they'd planned to eat in Port Jefferson, making no attempt to housekeep until the gas and electricity were turned on tomorrow. The prospect of a fifty-four-mile round trip over dark, unfamiliar roads seemed untenable however, particularly when there were enough fruit and crackers left over from a snack stop that afternoon.

They had made a simple meal of these, sitting in front of the fire and chatting.

"I bet Linda and Bill would enjoy it here," Ellen said.

"I'm sure they would," he grunted in amusement. "Though I doubt if Bill would much enjoy driving twenty-seven miles over back country roads to a hospital."

"No." After several moments, Ellen's smile faded. "I hope the baby isn't born while we're gone," she said.

"You told her to keep her legs crossed till we got back, didn't you?"

Ellen made no reply and, glancing over, David noted that her smile was one of wistful melancholy. He wondered if it troubled her to be the mother of a young woman shortly to become a mother herself. Not that Ellen ever indicated anything but pleasure at the thought; still, it was an unavoidable reminder of her age.

He settled back against the sofa cushion. The impetus of conversation seemed to have dissolved; probably, because of the silence and the somnific flickering of the fire. Fixing his gaze, he stared at the flames until darkness blotted in around him. It was as though he sat at one end of a long, black tunnel, at the other end of which the fire burned. Gradually, consciousness began to fade, the darkness penetrating to his mind. He hovered on the murky edge of sleep, doing nothing to avert the plunge. Weight suffused his eyelids, they started drooping.

"Honey?"

David's legs retracted jerkingly; he hitched around to look at her.

"You going to sleep?"

"No, no." He fought away a yawn. "What's on your mind?"

"I was just wondering if you'd care to take a little walk before we go to bed."

"Yeah," he said. "A good idea."

Five minutes later, they had left the house and walking toward the water, crunching sand beneath their high-top shoes. "Which way?" David asked.

"Well . . ." Ellen pointed speculatively toward the distant bluff. "That way?"

"I see nothing against it."

Ellen linked her arm with his. "Then that's the way we'll go," she said.

"We'll have to take a nice, long hike tomorrow, bring a picnic lunch along," he said.

"That would be fun."

They said no more and David lapsed into an almost thoughtless reverie, the rhythmic crunching of their shoes along the sand and the recurrent boom and hiss of the surf acting, on him, like a narcotic. Soon he was aware of no particular emotion, his mind suspended in an undiscerning void. When, finally, she spoke, he didn't hear the words and, starting, glanced at her. "Mmm?"

"This is what we did that first night," she repeated.

David registered the words but not their meaning. First night? Nearly fifteen seconds passed before it came to him that she was referring to their honeymoon. "That's right," he said, "we did."

Silence again; with it, a burden of renewed despondency on David's mind. Was it really going to work? Could they make it work after what had happened?

"There's that mansion," Ellen said.

David blinked, refocusing, and tilted back his head to look at the summit of the bluff ahead. The upper stories of the house were visible against the sky, lamp light in one of its windows. "I wonder who does live there," he said.

"Whoever it is, they're probably in Europe now," she said. "Or Hawaii."

"Good God, you think it might be just their summer place?"

"It might." Ellen pulled up the collar of her jacket, shivering.

"Cold?" he asked.

"A little."

"Want to go back?"

"Let's walk a little further."

"Okay."

Shortly afterward, they reached the foot of the bluff to find themselves blocked because the tide was in. They stopped and David draped his arm across her shoulders as they watched the breakers. For a while, he tried to think of something they could talk about but, finally, gave it up. There was no help for it; he simply couldn't overcome this feeling of inert detachment. But was it his or hers?

"I guess we both could use a good night's sleep," Ellen said, at last.

"We could at that," he heard himself reply. "We'll walk some more tomorrow."

While Ellen was washing and brushing her teeth—earlier, he'd managed to turn on the water—David kindled a fire in the bedroom, then stood before it, taking off his clothes as rapidly as possible and donning his pajamas; he was grateful, now, that Ellen had persuaded him to bring along a pair of woolen ones. Scuttling over the icy floorboards, he yanked back an edge of bedclothes and squeezed beneath them, hissing at the coldness of the sheets. He thrashed his legs to warm them, then sat, arms crossed, shivering fitfully as he looked around the quiet room.

He wondered when the house was built, deciding that it couldn't have been later than the early thirties. It was not too unattractive a place, really; this room was rather nice, in fact. Like the dining alcove and, to a lesser degree, the living room, it had a quality of tasteful organization about it.

Reaching out, he pulled open the bedside table drawer and looked inside. It was empty except for a box of incense called *Amour Exotica;* the name made David smile. Lifting off the cover, he sniffed at one of the shriveled, umber cakes inside, grimacing at the odor.

He replaced the cover, dropped the box into its drawer and pushed the drawer shut. Twisting around, he started to prop one of the pillows against the headboard when he noticed a row of five, time-worn X's scratched on the wood. He wondered who had put them there. A woman, probably; men were not inclined toward this symbol for the kiss. A young woman—perhaps a girl; a honeymooner even. Turning back, David slumped against the pillow, visualizing her in this bed with her new husband. They had just made love and were lying, side by side, in cozy indolence, legs entwined, the man's arms wrapped around her warm, soft body. Now the woman reached back languidly and, with her fingernail—or a bobby pin or the stone of her engagement ring—scribed an X on the headboard, then another and another until all five were there.

Done, she gave her husband a smile of drowsy contentment and, cuddling close to him, fell sound asleep.

In the fireplace, a chunk of wood broke loose and tumbled to the grate. David started and turned, starting again as he saw that Ellen stood, immobile, in the doorway, looking at him; he wondered how long she'd been there. "What are you doing?" he asked.

"Nothing." Ellen smiled elusively and crossed the room. She set the candle holder on the bedside table and began removing her bathrobe. She wrinkled up her nostrils. "What's that smell?" she asked, grimacing.

"Amour Exotica," he answered.

"What?" Her smile was tentative.

"Incense." He pointed. "In the bedside table drawer."

"Oh." She draped her robe across the footrail, moved around the bed and shucked her slippers to crawl across the spread and get beneath the covers with him. "Oh, my God," she said, "it's like sliding in between two sheets of ice."

"It's warmer over here," he told her.

"I don't want to get you cold."

"Don't be silly."

"Well . . ." Ellen shifted toward him gingerly, the touch of her chilled feet against his ankles making him jump. "I'm sorry," she said.

He tried not to wince at the constant, icy pressure of her feet. Reaching up, he buttoned shut the neck of her blue and white ski pajamas, conscious of how boyish in appearance Ellen was, at that moment, her small bust inconspicuous beneath the loose, woolen folds, her dark, blonde hair cropped short.

After she was warm, he drew aside the bedclothes and, standing, headed for the bathroom. "Brush my teeth," he said.

"Won't you need the candle?" Ellen asked.

"Oh; yeah." Turning back, David hurried to the table and picked up the candle holder. "God, this floor is cold!" He started toward the hall again, then side-tracked to the bureau and, shifting rapidly from foot to foot, fumbled through the contents of the suitcase, looking for his slippers. Finding them, he put them on and turned for the doorway. "Be back," he said. She didn't answer and he glanced across his shoulder at her. "You be here?"

She nodded, smiling. "Brush 'em good," she told him.

When he returned, Ellen was lying with her back turned to him. David set the candle holder on the table, kicked off his slippers and slid beneath the bedclothes hastily; the intense chill of the bathroom had penetrated to his bones, it seemed. Lying down, he shuddered violently several times, then started warming. Shortly afterward, he drew his left hand from beneath the covers, licked the tips of his thumb and index finger and pinched the burning wick.

He lay still for almost half a minute, then pushed up onto his right elbow to lean over and kiss the side of Ellen's neck. "Good night," he said. The bedclothes rustled as she stirred; her palm stroked once across his hair.

"Night," she murmured.

For a while—to him, it seemed, at least an hour—David lay on his back, eyes closed, waiting for sleep to come. God knows I'm tired enough, he thought repeatedly. With all the details of preparing for the trip, the pace of the last three days had been frenetic. Now, all of it had reached fruition; they were here, the stimulation of incessant activity ended. It seemed logical to assume that he would sleep, having slept so meagerly in the past week. Oppressively enough, the opposite seemed true.

David opened his eyes and looked at the wavering reflection of fire on the ceiling. Outside, the breakers crashed resoundingly; more loudly with each passing minute, he imagined. Why had he always assumed that the sound of surf conduced relaxing? Obviously, it didn't. The booming of the waves was unsettling to him; as if he were attempting to rest while lying in the vicinity of periodically fired cannons. He twisted sluggishly onto his right side. Great if he didn't sleep all week, he thought; he'd make a fine companion.

"Can't you sleep either?" Ellen asked.

David started in surprise. "You're still awake?"

"Mm-hmm."

"What's wrong?"

She hesitated. "I don't know. Maybe I'm cold."

He hesitated several moments, then shifted over to her. "Here," he said. He put his left arm across her. "Lie against me."

"I don't want to keep you from sleeping."

"You won't."

"You're sure?"

"Yes," he said. "Come on."

"Okay." Ellen huddled back against him. Except for her feet, she seemed almost hot to David. He smiled, thinking how uncanny it was that a woman could feel so warm and still be cold.

He closed his eyes and tried to sleep, then, as Ellen snuggled closer to him, realized that, from force of habit, he had cupped his hand over her right breast; he could feel, through her pajama top, the nipple hardening against his palm. Soon, the nape of her neck came in contact with his lips and he kissed it automatically. Ellen writhed a little, sighing. David felt his body tensing, and he pushed against her harder. Almost independently, it seemed, his fingers slid beneath the bottom edge of her pajama top, eased up across her ribs and gripped themselves around her breast again. Kneading tautly at the flesh, he began to roll her erected nipple between two fingers. Ellen drew in laboring breath.

"I'm going to try. I really am," she said.

A wave of coldness seemed to pass across David and he stopped caressing her.

"I told you it wouldn't be easy," she said.

He sighed. Be reasonable, he told himself. "I understand," he said.

"I'm still a little . . . shaky, David." She was silent for a few moments, then spoke again. "I'm going to try, that's all I can say."

David kissed her on the cheek. "Okay," he said. "I'll wait."

She put a hand on his and squeezed it. "Thank you," she murmured.

After a while, very slowly, she began to inch away from him. He pretended he was sleeping when it happened.

He thought he might have slept; he wasn't sure. Time had lost its continuity and he couldn't tell how long afterward it was that Ellen stirred. Perhaps it was her movement that awakened him. Opening his eyes, he watched her draw covertly from him, sitting up. "What's wrong?" he mumbled.

"Oh; I'm sorry, I didn't mean to wake you."

"What's wrong?" he asked.

"Nothing."

"Why are you sitting up then?"

"Oh . . ." She looked unsure. "I thought I'd take a walk."

"Now?"

She didn't answer but, after several moments, stood, hissing at the coldness of the floorboards. As she felt around, located and put on her slippers, David pushed up on his right elbow, watching her groggily. Ellen glanced at him and he wondered if he saw, in the uncertain light, a smile flicker across her lips. "Go back to sleep," she told him.

"Don't you think you ought to get some rest yourself?"

"I will, in a while." Ellen gathered up her clothes and shoes and, lighting the candle, started for the hall.

"You want me to go with you?" he asked.

"No, no; rest," she answered.

He watched until she'd gone into the hall, then, as the bathroom door closed, slumped back on his pillow. He visualized her dressing in the chill silence of the bathroom, her shadow gelatinous on the walls and ceiling. Hell, he thought.

Sighing wearily, he turned onto his left side and stared at the fire. It was burning steadily, short yellow flames licking up around the chunk of driftwood like demon tongues. The idea occurred to him that, actually, Ellen planned to take a drive. He smiled in rueful amusement, envisioning her driving to the airport and flying back to Los Angeles without him. That'd be a merry prank, he thought.

His gaze shifted toward the doorway as Ellen left the bathroom and started down the stairs. You sure you don't want me to go with you? he imagined himself calling after her. Then: How long will you be gone? Finally: Be careful! By the time he had considered speaking each of them aloud, the front door had thumped shut and she was gone. David rolled onto his back with a sigh.

A short while later, he exhaled surrenderingly and, sitting up, threw aside the covers. For several moments he sat immobile, eyes closed, then with a mumbling groan, slipped his legs across the mattress edge, wincing as the soles of his feet touched the floorboards. Standing, he donned his robe and slippers, an idea presenting itself to mind: to go downstairs and make some coffee; be waiting, on her return, with a full, steaming pot of it plus a blazing fire in the living room. The notion vanished in an instant. That's a great idea, he thought, except there's no coffee and no way of making any.

He looked around. Well, he could have a fire waiting for her anyway; some toasted cracker crumbs, he thought, smiling to himself. He'd make the gesture anyway. He turned for the hall. Need a candle, he thought. No, he didn't; he could find his way without one.

Darkness pressed against his eyes as he left the bedroom, feeling to his right until he found the bannister rail. Brushing fingertips along the frigid surface of the wood, he scuffed his way to the stairs, turned right and started down. As he descended, he reached up with his left hand and held together the edges of his robe.

He was starting across the studio landing when a narrow bar of light suddenly appeared on the floor in front of him. Recoiling with a gasp, he stared at it obtusely for a few seconds before turning his head to see that he'd left the door enough ajar that afternoon to admit the light. Swallowing, he stepped to the door and pushed it open.

The light was from the moon; it must have left obscuring clouds precisely at the moment he had reached the landing. David looked across the broad expanse of floor which seemed to have been gilded with a coat of luminous paint. After several moments, he walked across the studio to the windows.

The view was startling. The entire beach had the cast of faded silver and, even though the surf was more than a hundred yards distant, the crash and frothing dissolution of each wave was astonishingly visible. David's gaze followed the sinuous line of moonlight reflected on the Sound until it receded into blackness.

He looked to the right and left, trying to see her—but she was out of sight. That or his vision wasn't strong enough to pick her out at any substantial distance. He closed his eyes to rest them. Probably need glasses, he thought.

He wondered what he should really do. Remain here, staring emptily at sand and sea? Go downstairs to poke and feed the fire back to life? Or go back to bed? He remained immobile, unable to decide.

He never knew how long he had been under observation. All he knew was that, abruptly, he was conscious of being watched and turned to see a figure standing in the doorway. "I thought you were going for a walk," he said.

There was no reply.

"Well?"

Still no reply. David frowned. "Aren't you even going to talk to me?" he asked.

The figure stood in silence.

"Ellen?" There was something else beside annoyance in his voice now; a tendril of disquiet. "What's the matter?"

His breath caught as a young woman took a step into the moonlight, staring at him. As initial shock declined, David saw that she was the most beautiful woman he'd ever seen in his life, her shoulder-length hair jet black, her features perfect, carved as if from ivory. She wore a pale white skirt and sweater set, a chain and locket at her throat. Her feet were bare and flaked with sand.

David swallowed. "Can I help you?" he heard himself inquire.

The woman murmured. "Terry?"

David looked at her confusedly. When she spoke the name a second time, he answered, "No, I'm sorry. I'm—"

He broke off, shuddering, at the sound she made— part sob, part convulsive inhalation. For a moment, he thought she was going to cry.

"You . . . live around here?" he asked.

The woman's dark eyes held on his. She didn't answer.

"Miss?"

Her eyelids fell shut as though to block away the sight of him, her expression, now, one of bitter disappointment. For almost thirty seconds, she stood motionless and still, enveloped by an obvious grief. Then she opened her eyes and looked at him again. "I live down the beach," she said, "around the bluff." She came a few steps closer to him, staring at his face as if to verify, to herself, that he was not the man she sought. David grew uncomfortable beneath her intense surveillance.

Suddenly, she smiled and he caught his breath a second time, the effect was so startling. Since his early twenties, he had not reacted in such a way to sheer, physical beauty—with a binding at the throat, a palpable stagger of the heart. The woman was exquisite, her beauty that of dreams.

"I'm sorry," she said, "I didn't mean to stare at you."

"And I'm—" He stopped in consternation, finding himself about to say: And I'm sorry that I'm not Terry. He cleared his throat. "—Wondering what you're doing here," he finished awkwardly.

"I saw firelight upstairs," the woman said, "and I thought—" For a moment, sorrow flickered on her face; then she smiled again. "I knew the artist who lived here last summer," she explained. "I was out walking and I saw the firelight and thought—he's back."

David nodded, staring. When she said no more, he twitched as if emerging from a reverie, feeling gauche for having gaped at her like a bedazzled school boy. "And his name was Terry," he said, speaking the first words that came to mind.

"Yes," she answered, "Terry Lawrence."

"I see." He was beginning to nod vacantly again. *Dear God, but she was beautiful.* He twitched a second time, struggling for poise. "Is he the one who did those paintings downstairs?" he asked, deliberately. "The one over the mantel; the miniatures on the stairwell?"

The woman nodded. "Yes; aren't they good?"

"Very good. I was saying to my—" David hesitated for an instant, then, recognizing that it was reluctance to mention Ellen which motivated the pause, continued self-reprovingly, "—wife this afternoon how interesting they are."

The woman gazed at him fixedly, making him swallow. Finally, she said, "I'm sorry I keep staring at you. It's just that you remind me so of Terry."

He could neither rationalize nor overcome the surge of pleasure he experienced at her words. Instantly, his mind was jumbled with a chaos of jejune replies and he found himself torn between the habit of shunning any lapse in personal taste and the compulsion to voice the phrases nonetheless.

She spared him the necessity of decision by asking, "Don't you want to know my name?"

"*Yes;* of course." Was that really his voice he heard; so throaty, so affected?

The woman walked over to him, extending her right hand which, in the moonlight, looked almost opalescent. "I'm Marianna," she said.

As in a dream, David held the hand in his, so close to her now that he gave up trying to resist the urge to stare.

"What is it?" she asked.

"You're—"

"—what?"

He drew in halting breath. There seemed no way of avoiding the particular words. As near to him as she was, her skin and features were like flawless marble.

"You're very beautiful," he said.

Marianna's grip tightened slowly and he had the

sensation of his fingers coalescing with hers. She spoke but it was only incoherent sound to him. "What?" he murmured.

"You haven't told me *your* name," she repeated.

"Oh." He winced embarrassedly. "I'm sorry. It's David." For some reason, it seemed extraneous to mention last names. David and Marianna were quite enough.

He realized that he was still holding her hand and, with a diffident smile, released it, scouring his mind for some appropriate remark. "So you . . . thought Terry Lawrence was back," he said.

She nodded. "I've been waiting for him."

"You're not in touch with him then," he said, hoping that his curiosity was not as obvious as it seemed.

Marianna shook her head.

Good, he thought; it startled him to note how instantly. He smiled as though to mitigate the flash of unwarranted reaction. Her returned smile made him shiver, it illumined her face with such a radiance. "Would you like to see a painting he did of me?" she asked.

He was just aware of nodding. "Yes," he said.

"Come along then."

He couldn't take his gaze away from her as she took his hand and started guiding him across the studio. There are certain human beings, he thought, whom nature has created so consummately that they have been accorded the status of art objects. Marianna was one of these.

"Why do you look at me like that?" she asked.

David flinched, realizing that, somehow, he had deluded himself into thinking her unaware of his scrutiny. Momentarily, he tried to think of some politic lie, then gave it up. "Don't all men look at you like that?" he asked.

Her reaction was an unexpected one. Stopping, she turned to face him, grasping his other hand as well. "Look then," she said.

For a moment, he resisted, some dormant inhibition cautioning him; then surrendering, he looked at her without restraint, moving a candid gaze across the separate elements of her face—her forehead and her eyes, her nose and ears, her cheeks, her lips, her chin—then relishing the perfection of their blend. As moments passed, he started to acquire an almost irresistible craving to lean forward and press his face against her ebony hair, to kiss her cheek, even take her lips with forceful greed. Abruptly, he drew his hands away, just able to murmur, "I guess I'd better stop now."

"Why?"

"Because—" He blinked and shook himself. "Well, because—" The only phrase his mind could invoke was: Because I am a married man, and he rejected that as too baroquely corny even for consideration. "Just because," he settled for. "Show me your painting."

Marianna gazed at him with childlike curiosity, then returned his smile, bewitching him again. "All right," she said and led him to a wall.

David looked at her. "This is it?"

"Mmm-hmm."

A fragmentary dread oppressed him; that she wasn't quite as rational as she seemed. Her teasing smile assuaged the doubt. David repressed his own smile and said, "I see a wall."

"Yes, so do I," she said. Looking at him with the

impish smile, she felt along the paneling until some-thing clicked and, where the wall had been unbroken, a door now stood ajar. "There," she said.

David peered inside. "What's in there?"

Marianna moved into the darkness. "Come and see," her voice invited.

Something in her tone reacted on his body like an excitant and, suddenly, he felt desire coursing through him like a fuming wine. He began to speak, realized that his throat was parched and swallowed, clearing it. "All right," he answered, following her.

Silence. Blackness pulsing at his eyes. David squinted, trying, in vain, to pick out Marianna's sil-houette.

"Where are you?" he asked.

She didn't answer. David reached out with both his hands, groping for her like a blind man. "Marianna?"

"Here," she said.

David tightened as the words *I want you* flared across his mind. Watch it, he thought; he was allowing himself to be misled by this quasi-romantic atmo-sphere. "Where?" he asked, a tinge of self-willed impa-tience in his voice.

Suddenly, her hand was grasping his, her presence engulfing him again, drawing at him with a magnetism he could, almost, feel. Part of him shrank from it in prudent apprehension but another part wanted to pull her to himself in savage wantonness, embrace her vio-lently, take her lips, demand—

"What is it?" Marianna asked, as he shuddered.

He drew in stifled breath. "Where's the painting?" he asked.

"You really want to see it?"

It was, the way she said it, practically an invitation.

He could see no other possible interpretation. Closing his eyes, David tried to disengage his hand from hers, appalled at the erratic flutter of his breathing. "Yes," he said. "Where is it?"

Marianna's hand let go and the all but viable current ceased to flow between them; a tide of coldness seemed to cover David. "Right over here," she told him.

"I'd better light a match," he said.

"Is your wife angry with you?"

David started. "What?"

"When you thought I was her, you said: Aren't you even going to talk to me?"

He blinked, remembering. "Oh."

"Have you been arguing?"

"Well . . ." He felt inclined to snap: What business is it of yours? but couldn't bring himself to do so. He stood in hapless silence.

"Never mind," Marianna told him in a subdued voice, "you don't have to tell me."

Instinctively, he reached out in the dark to take her hand and reassure her, then, stiffening with reaction, checked the movement, pulled out the book of matches he'd found on the bedroom mantel and struck one. It didn't work and he had to use a second one. Marianna averted her face from the leap of flame, her expression one of momentary pain.

When she looked back at him, David felt the drawing tingle in his flesh again, stronger than ever now. It was almost unbelievable that any woman could be so lovely. He stared at her, imprisoned by her beauty.

"There's the painting," Marianna said, pointing. From the way she smiled, it was obvious that she knew his feeling and he turned away, resentful, yet, at the same time, reluctant to remove his eyes from her.

From what he could see in the imperfect light, the painting had not captured all her grace; but the essence was there, the—he stumbled briefly for the word—spirit. David nodded slowly, unaware that he was doing so. He raised the match to see better. For an instant, the singularity of it all struck him—standing in a musty storage room with this woman in the middle of the night, gazing at her portrait by the flickering glow of a match flame—then, the notion vanished and, once more, he was isolated in wordless homage to her beauty.

"Do you like it?" Marianna asked.

"It's very good," he said. "When did he paint it?"

"Last summer."

He lit another match and kept looking at the portrait, nodding. It showed only Marianna's head and shoulders. Did he ever paint you in the nude? the question sprang to mind. He restrained it, loathe to consider the thought; why, he had no idea. It was implausible that he should feel possessive toward a woman he had known no longer than ten to fifteen minutes. It was her beauty, of course, he realized then. To view it was to covet it.

He turned back. "Well, it certainly—"

He broke off, seeing that he was alone. Startled, he moved to the doorway in the wall and back into the studio. Marianna stood at the windows, looking out. David shook out the match. "Shall I close the door?" he asked.

"I guess," she answered, sounding vague and apathetic. David felt a pang of concern. Without knowing why, he was conscious of a need to please her. Keeping his gaze on her face, he reached back and pushed the wall door shut, then moved over to where she stood.

She did not acknowledge his presence. David winced unconsciously. Her remoteness was unsettling to him. Several minutes ago, their rapport had been complete. Now she seemed withdrawn beyond reach. Impotently, he searched his mind for something which might bring her back. "That's a—pretty locket you're wearing," he said, finally.

She turned to face him and, although he strained to curb the reaction, her affectionate smile sent renewed pleasure through him. "Would you like to look at it?" she asked.

"Very much." Momentarily, he saw himself, a character in some improbable television drama, mouthing lines bestowed upon him by some unseen—and highly unaccomplished—writer. The vision was eclipsed as Marianna reached behind her neck with both hands and he noted, almost with a start, the imposing swell of her breasts. Swallowing, he took the circular locket from her hand and looked at it. In the moonlight, he could see that it was gold, with a jewel in its center. He looked at her. "Diamond?"

"Yes," she said. "Terry gave it to me."

He nodded, smiling, doing it, he sensed, as he had described in far too many scripts: *bravely*. "He must love you very much," he said.

Marianna turned from him abruptly. "He doesn't love me at all," she said. "If he did, he wouldn't have left."

David stared at her, as pleased as he was caught off balance; he'd expected anything but this. He started then as Marianna turned and headed for the door. "I have to leave," she said.

"But—" David broke off, strickenly, realizing that

he had no right to voice the words which filled his mind: When will I see you again?

"Goodbye," she said.

Right hand raised impulsively, David started after her, then, once more, checked himself. He had no justification whatever to follow Marianna. The knowledge filled him with a sense of crippling loss as he watched her leave the studio and turn left to go down the staircase. In a while, still listening, motionless, he heard the front door shut and drew in sudden breath. Turning, he moved back to the windows, hoping to catch sight of her outside.

There was nothing. Time passed and there was only empty, moonlit beach before him. David's shoulders slumped. He stood there several minutes longer, then, with a weary sigh, trudged across the studio, closing the door behind him as he left. He felt depleted. The ascent to the bedroom seemed as arduous a labor as he'd ever undertaken.

It was not until he'd sat down heavily on the bed that he felt the locket in his hand. He stared at it a few minutes, dismally, then, on impulse, began to pry his thumbnail in between the halves, thinking that they might be separate; he flinched as they sprang ajar. Lighting another match, he looked at the right-hand photograph. He frowned. He didn't look, at all, like Terry. His gaze shifted to Marianna's face.

The sound he made appalled him. It was such a sound as youth might make when suffering the unexpected onslaught of love.

FRIDAY

David opened his eyes and gazed up drowsily at the ceiling. For a while, he lay immobile, listening to the muffled detonations of the surf; then he turned his head to look at Ellen. Immediately, he started up in troubled surprise. She wasn't there. It looked as if she hadn't slept there either.

Stripping back the bed clothes, he dropped his legs across the mattress edge and, standing, hurried to the nearest dormer window. The car was gone. David stared down blankly at its tire tracks, feeling the throb of a vein at his temple. Abruptly, he turned and started for the hall. Halfway there, he saw a scrap of paper leaned against the bedside table lamp and moved to get it.

Didn't want to wake you up. Have gone to Port Jefferson to check on gas and electricity and pur-chase goodies for the tum. Start fire, have faith and look for the return of—yr. obt. Ellen.

David smiled affectionately at the note, then, a second later, shivered in reaction. For a moment there, he'd actually been afraid that she'd left him. Thus the measure of my confidence, he thought, grimacing.

He realized how cold his feet were getting and, sitting on the bed, donned his slippers. Checking his watch, he saw that it was just past nine o'clock. He must have gone to sleep the moment he'd hit the bed last night. He hadn't meant to; not with such an intriguing—and ice-breaking—anecdote to tell.

Then, again,—he frowned, attempting to remember—had he really meant to tell Ellen at that time? As he recalled, his attitude, on returning from the studio, had been one of somewhat glassy-eyed infatuation. Under such a circumstance, it was, perhaps, as well that he had toppled off before Ellen's arrival. She might have discerned a sound of misguided rapture in his voice—which wouldn't have helped a hell of a lot to alleviate their discord.

While he dressed, his skin rippled with gooseflesh, David looked out through the dormer window. The morning was grey and sunless and the wind had risen again. *Come to Romantic Logan Beach in the Frostbite Season,* he thought. What an idiot he'd been to suggest this trip. A week in Palm Springs would have served as well.

He was putting on his shirt when Marianna's chain and locket spilled to the floor. As he picked it up, he realized that, until the second it had fallen, he had been rather inclined to appraise last night's amourette as, at least, imagined, at most, hallucinated. Now, in an instant, he was obliged to face the fact that Marianna really did exist. But, surely, she could not be near as beautiful as—impulsively, he parted the locket halves and looked to verify his doubt.

He shook his head dumbfoundedly. Dear God, she

was; fully as beautiful as he remembered. For once, memory had not exaggerated. Only after a long while was he able to remove his gaze to look at Terry's photograph. Here was the discrepancy. How Marianna could, possibly, say that he reminded her of this man was beyond understanding. He had darkish-blond hair whereas Terry's was as black as Marianna's. His face was ruddy and full, Terry's sallow and lean and—he thought, with uncharitable amusement—rather vulpine, to boot.

Further, from the unfocalized cast of Terry's eyes, he estimated that the painter wore corrective lenses—perhaps, exceptionally thick ones. David grunted, smiling. Terry was probably, also, five-foot two and scrawny whereas he was six-foot two and broad enough to pass for an active football player. All in all, a staggering resemblance, he thought; we're practically the Corsican Brothers.

His smile faded, disappearing, and he dropped the chain and locket back into the pocket of his shirt. He finished dressing, exited the bedroom and, following a bathroom stop, went downstairs to the living room.

He stopped as he saw the blanket on the sofa; this was where she'd spent the night then. David winced. She must have been more distressed than he'd supposed. He wondered if she'd left the blanket there as an accusing reminder, then decided that such a suspicion was unworthy of him. Folding the blanket, he dropped it onto an armchair. Poor kid must have frozen even so, the thought occurred. His smile was rueful. *Kid*, he thought; hope springs sappily eternal. Middle-aged men announce the advent of evenings out with "the boys": middle-aged women schedule bridge sets with "the girls". He shook his head. This is the forefront of the hottest battle, he thought: mankind vs. calendar.

Once the fire was burning steadily, a sense of restlessness began oppressing him. He tried to deflect it by calculating the probable length of Ellen's trip. Port Jefferson was twenty-seven slow miles away. That meant a total of fifty-four miles plus whatever time and mileage would be required to shop for food. David groaned, dejectedly. He might, as well, have foregone calculations; they only aggravated his unrest. Ellen might have left a few minutes before he'd woken up; she might be absent for hours.

What was he to do? He could try fishing but it wouldn't be very enjoyable on an empty stomach. Read? He made a disgruntled face. That had no appeal whatever. David sighed, capitulating; that left walking. So he'd walk.

A minute later, he was in his jacket, trudging away from the house and sniffing at the air so vigorously it dizzied him. Air of such exhilarating purity was one feature the San Fernando Valley couldn't match. Residing there, one, actually, forgot the smell of truly fresh air, one grew so accustomed to the caustic flavor of the smog. Now if only he had an ample breakfast tucked away, he could really look forward to an extended hike along the beach.

As he angled toward the water, he lay back his head and stared at the overcast sky. Sure as hell looks like rain, he thought; but, then, it had looked like rain yesterday too. That was California adaptation again. As an ex-resident of New York City, his remembrance of eastern rain had, no doubt, been distorted by the fact that rainfall in Los Angeles was so limited. Obviously, it didn't rain here every time a cloud appeared; he'd just brainwashed himself into recalling that it did. Lowering his gaze, he looked across the choppy, blue-grey surface of the Sound, then at the desolate strand of beach ahead, thinking: What could be more barren than a summer colony in the winter?

He was near the bluff now and he looked up at the house on top of it. Who *did* live there? he wondered. It was an imposing structure; and what an overwhelming view it must afford. Writers really should inhabit houses like that, he thought; puttering around in smoking jackets, puffing learnedly at pipes and pondering on major novels all of which are destined for morocco bindings. There was something inappropriately arid about his neat, clean, modern house in Sherman Oaks; something alien to creativity.

He shook himself, grimacing to frighten off disheartening reflections. Not today, he thought. He concentrated on the great house on the bluff, envisioning its occupants—a retired magnate with a burnished pate, vast annuities and a withered, snowy-haired spouse who tapped about the mansion with a silver-tipped cane. No, a retired diva, goddess of the Continent during Queen Victoria's reign, now alone with faded gowns and memories and aged Babette, her loyal if disintegrating French retainer. Horse shit, David thought; he'd been dealing in cliches too long. Probably, the owner of a hardware store lived up—

His thought broke off abruptly as he saw the figure of a woman standing near the edge of the bluff, close by the top of a wooden step construction which led down to the beach. He hadn't noticed her sooner because she stood beneath the shading of a pine tree. Walking steadily, David stared at her. Was it Marianna? He couldn't tell but the impression he received was that of an older woman; he noted the erratic flutter of a wind-whipped scarf at her neck.

He frowned at himself. It could hardly be Marianna. She'd told him she lived down the beach around the bluff. He kept staring at the woman as he walked. Was she watching him? Again, he couldn't tell. Perhaps she was; what difference did it make? Things were probably so slow around here that the sight of a new man moving on the beach might have made her day. David smiled and shook his head, lowering his gaze.

The tide was out and, as he rounded the base of the almost vertical bluff, threading a path between mussel-scabbed boulders, he caught sight of a cottage about half a mile down the beach. She really *does* live here, the thought appeared, unbidden, startling him. He hadn't been aware of doubting it and yet he must have. Why? he wondered. Had he felt, subconsciously, that she'd lied to him in order not to see him again?

Reaching hard-packed sand, he started walking faster, trying, in vain, to ignore the obvious acceleration of his heartbeat. Ambivalent emotions tore at him. On one hand, he decried his adolescent eagerness to see Marianna again. At the same time, the very existence of this eagerness was gratifying to him. He was forty-six years old, by God, and had given up the hope of ever feeling this particular zeal again.

He thrust aside the undesired notion by inventing a scene between Marianna and himself as she opened the door to his knock. He held up the locket, smiling. She said, "Well, hello," delightedly. She was alone, of course. Resourceful fancy would allow no other odds—unless it might permit the presence of a bed-ridden granny in the attic, a night-working father insensibly asleep. Hell, no, he re-evaluated, she's alone. Her entire family died in a hurricane. And she made wonderful coffee.

So engrossed was he in quixotic images that he'd almost reached the cottage before noticing that its shutters were closed, that it had, about it, a patina of long disuse. Frowning puzzledly, he increased his pace, walking as fast as caution would allow; after all, she *might* be there and notice his approach. It took no more than moments, though, to realize that the cottage could not have been occupied for years—or, if it had, its occupant had no regard whatever for appearances. That hardly tallied with his image of Marianna.

To double-check, he knocked repeatedly on both front and rear doors but would have been astounded had she answered. He walked around the cottage several times, only then allowing himself to accept the demeaning realization that she had lied to him. Clearly, she had never lived here, and there was no other house in sight except for the mansion on the bluff. Was it possible she lived there? That the woman he'd seen had really been her after all? David sighed. What did it matter where she lived? Obviously, she had no desire to see him again.

As he trudged back toward the house, his mind kept bringing up the phrase: *He felt his years.* At first, it only made him smile in somber resignation, then it irritated him. Finally, he forced himself to concentrate on other things, reduced, at length, to counting boulders in order to suppress the thought. Even so, it appeared whenever he relaxed his vigil; felt his years. He felt his years. He—"Oh, shut up!" he ordered his infuriating mind. You're here to make up with Ellen.

Stop forgetting that, he thought.

*   *   *

The green-flecked wave curved over, hung in beetling suspension for an instant, then toppled to destruction. Shapeless fragments of it leaped into the air, its main bulk gushing up the sandy inclination, a carpet of swirling foam which stopped, held momentarily, then was suctioned back to lose identity beneath the ponderous fall of the next, incoming wave.

David stood, statue-like, gazing at the endless ranks of whitecaps rolling in. When he heard the faint voice calling from behind, he started convulsively and turned around. Ellen was standing by the house. David raised his arm and waved, conscious of a sudden need for her. He started forward, glancing at his watch. It was ten minutes past eleven.

"Hi," she said as he came up to her.

"Hi." David kissed her on the cheek and hugged her with his right arm. "I'm glad you're back." He kissed a corner of her lips.

His welcome seemed, momentarily, confusing to her; then, smiling, she took his hand and squeezed it. "Want to help me unload the car?"

"You bet."

They started along the side of the house, David's arm across her shoulders. "Cold today," he said.

"Yes. It's nice though." Ellen glanced at him. "What have you been doing?" she asked.

"Walking mostly."

"Did you have a good sleep?"

"Fine," he said. "Did you?"

"Yes," she answered in a tone which indicated that she hadn't but was trying to be pleasant about it. David considered mentioning her sleeping in the living room, then decided against it. Let it lie, he thought. The

situation was resolved now; no point in touching it off
again. "When did you leave?" he asked.

"A little before nine."

He nodded. "Gas and electricity today?"

"By this afternoon."

"Good."

"You must be starving."

He had to think about it. "Yeah; I am," he said,
amazed that he could have overlooked it. "Ravenous."

"I'll make you a nice, big platter of scrambled eggs."

"I'll eat it. Wait a second. How can you if the gas
isn't turned on yet?"

"Fireplaces were invented before stoves."

"So they were," he said, smiling.

They reached the car and David pulled open the
right door. He eyed the array of food in the two card-
board cartons on the front seat: eggs, bread, crackers,
coffee, margarine, cheese, luncheon meat, soup. He
straightened up, lifting one of the cartons. "That stuff
looks good," he said.

Ellen patted his back. "I'll get your breakfast right
away."

He followed her through the front doorway. "Oh, the
fire's almost out," she said.

"I'll jazz it up."

"Not too high."

"No, ma'am."

She held open the kitchen door for him. "Think you
can eat six eggs?" she asked.

"Raw." He turned back toward the door.

When he returned to the kitchen with the second
carton of groceries, Ellen was removing, from a sack, a
bottle of Extra-Dry Martini Mix. She held it up and

David made a pleased expression. "The good ameni-ties," he said. He took the bottle from her and began to dig a nail beneath its neck wrapping. "How about you?" he asked.

"A little later."

"Sure?"

"After I cook."

"Okay."

He went into the living room with a tall glassful of martini and took sips from it as he fed and prodded the fire back to life.

Very quickly, the gin was doing things to him. Al-ready, the edges of his vision had blurred, the cotton padding been installed between reality and response. Who cares about Marianna? he thought. I'm here with Ellen Audrey. She's my sweetheart.

He turned as Ellen entered with a heavy, black skil-let and fork, a cube of margarine and a bowl of egg batter. "One side, soldier," she said.

"Sir!" He snapped to stiff attention, saluted, Brit-ish-style, and sidestepped.

"I note that your martini has prevailed," she said.

"Yes, sir, it has! Thank you for asking! May I stand at ease, sir?"

Ellen set the skillet down on top of the burning driftwood and started to unwrap the margarine. "If you can stand at all," she said.

"Buns to you, sir!" David sneezed explosively.

She looked at him, surprised. "You getting a cold?" she asked.

"I don't think so." Breaking off, he puckered up his face and sneezed again. "What the hell?" he said.

Ellen glanced down. "Your shoes are wet."

"Are they?" David looked at them. "Well, I'll be

damned; they are." Setting down his glass on the mantel, he lowered himself unsteadily to the raised hearth, propped the side of his right ankle on his left knee and began to untie his shoelace. His fingers felt a little numb. He dropped his shoe to the floor and, slowly, peeled off the sock. Movements, when drunk, are so beautifully protracted, he thought, so deliciously languid; or, at least, they seemed to be which was all that mattered anyway. Without impatience, one could foresee the removal of two shoes and a pair of socks as being an hour's undertaking.

He put down his right leg with leisurely aplomb, paused, then raised the left, depositing its ankle on the knee of his right leg. Well done, Cooper, he congratulated himself; splendidly negotiated. He untied his right shoelace with indolent carelessness and dropped it. Picking up his socks, he twisted around and wrung them out above the flames. "Hiss yourself," he told the fire.

"Good Lord," Ellen said, "how did you get them so wet?"

"I was wading."

Ellen grunted softly as she rocked the skillet. David watched the margarine cube slide hissingly from side to side, leaving a wake of golden brown froth. He tossed aside the wet clump of socks. "His laundry done, Mister Cooper now relaxes," he said, raising both legs in front of himself on the hearth and wrapping his arms around them. "He requests, of his devoted wife, that she discontinue melting ersatz butter long enough to return his extra-dry martini." He took the glass from her. "His loyal wife complies," he said. He raised the glass. "He offers a sip."

"I'd better do the eggs first."

David sighed. "Mr. Cooper contemplates the plight of the solitary drinker," he said. "He will—hey, you know that handle's going to get awfully hot."

"I know; I should have brought a pot holder." Ellen set down the skillet carefully, balancing it on the burning driftwood.

"I'll get you one," he said.

"No, not in your bare feet." She turned away and started for the kitchen.

As Ellen went into the kitchen, he looked around. Impulsively, he picked up the skillet and tilted it from side to side, making soft, whistling noises as what was left of the margarine cube skidded back and forth.

"Entertaining yourself?" she asked, when she got back.

"We seek what we can in the way of pleasures, yes." Abruptly, he let go of the skillet handle. "Yow!" he said, "that's hot!"

Ellen grabbed the skillet before it could fall. "You said it would be," she reminded him, repressing a smile.

"I never pay attention to myself."

"Getting hot in here," Ellen said.

He watched as she set down the skillet and took off her jacket, tossing it on top of the sofa. She poured egg batter into the skillet and began to stir with the fork. David watched her dully, all emotion in abeyance, his mind a leveled scale, waiting for the addition of weight on either side so it would tip the balance toward some specific attitude.

Ellen's leaning over seemed to do it. Suddenly, he found himself looking underneath her blouse at her left breast in its white brassiere cup. There was sudden traction in his groin and, as if all else had vanished, he stared at the breast, examining its shape and pendency, feeling, in his mind, the weight and warmth of it, its gelatinous give beneath the fingers.

"You looking at me?" Ellen asked.

"At your left breast."

She glanced at him to see if he was serious. "You really are?" she asked.

"I really are."

She grunted in bemusement. "Why?"

"Shhh. I'm looking."

After a while, Ellen let go of the fork and straightening up, undid the top two buttons of the blouse. "Be my guest," she said.

David shivered as Ellen leaned over again and the blouse hung free of both her breasts. He stared at them, imagining the feel of them as they were—the stitching of the cups against his fingertips, the taut swell of flesh beneath the lace—then, their appearance as it would be if he unhooked the brassiere and, suddenly unsupported, they fell by their own weight, the large, reddish-brown nipples exposed. Were they hardening now? Were they erect? The conjecture alone seemed of overwhelming stimulation to him. He could almost feel the fleshy hardness of them between his lips.

He glanced up to see her smiling at him. "Before eating?" she asked.

"Instead of eating?" he countered.

"That's extra-dry martini talking."

"Try me."

Ellen made a mock grim face. "You sound as though you mean business."

"I do." It was the strangest feeling of eroticism he could recall ever experiencing; to be somehow, irritated with her, yet to want her. Always before, he'd been incapable of even considering sex unless they were getting along. This emotion was entirely removed from personality. It disturbed him. Still, he was unable—unwilling, may be—to resist it. God knew they needed sex right now.

Abruptly, he bolted down his drink and stood. "By God, it *is* hot," he said, feeling a trickle of sweat across his chest. He set his glass down on the mantel and pulled off his jacket and sweater, tossing them on top of hers. "Why don't you take off your blouse?" he said.

Ellen looked at him appraisingly for several moments, then, without a word, put down the skillet and unbuttoned her blouse to the waist. She tugged the bottom portion from her slacks, until the last two buttons slipped it off her shoulders. David pulled it free and dropped it on the pile of clothing on the sofa. Ellen picked up the skillet again. "Better?" she asked.

Don't talk, he thought; he almost spoke the words aloud. "Better," he said. As though it were a separate entity, his right hand lifted to rub upward at the bottom of her right breast, then close around it, fingers flexing inward slowly. Ellen drew in sudden breath and he felt the breast swell tumidly against his palm, straining, for a moment, at its lace sheath. "If you want any breakfast—" she warned.

David didn't answer. Letting go, he slipped behind her and cupped a hand over each of her breasts, beginning to knead and fondle them.

"David—"

"Quiet." Bending over, he started to kiss her at the joint of her neck and shoulder, fingers massaging her bust. Ellen made a sound of faint distress but didn't try to stop him. He began to nibble at her neck, gently at first, then with more harshness.

"I can't make you proper scrambled eggs if you—"

She broke off as David bent over and disengaged her hand from the skillet handle. Taking the pot holder from her, he lifted the skillet from the fireplace and leaned over to put it on the hearth. As he did, the locket slipped from his pocket and fell to the floor.

"What's that?" Ellen asked. She picked it up to look at.

"Nothing," he murmured, trying to take it from her.

"No, really, what is it? she asked.

"Just . . . " He shrugged. "Some girl left it here," he told her.

"Girl?"

"Forget it." He slid his arms around her again. It doesn't matter, he thought. He tried to kiss her neck but she drew away.

"What girl?" she asked.

"I don't know," he said. He reached for her again. "She said she lives in a cottage down the beach but she doesn't."

He tried to take the locket from her again but she held on to it.

"When did you see her?" she asked. Her voice was tensing now.

He sighed. "Last night. Come on—"

She pulled away from him. "When?" she asked.

"While you were out walking," he said, trying to make it sound unimportant.

"I don't understand."

"Come on." He put his arms around her and started nuzzling her neck again. "There's nothing *to* understand, Ellen Audrey. She just came in, that's all. She used to know the artist who lived here."

Ellen was so still that he drew back to look at her. She stared at him, expressionless. He felt a tremor of irritation at the look but forced it away. "She saw firelight in the house and thought he was back. Now forget about her," he said.

"She just came in?"

"Yes." The irritation was in his voice now. "Will you please forget about her?"

Immediately, he regretted his tone. Her voice trembled slightly as she said, "You seem a little anxious for me to forget about her."

His smile was strained. "What?"

"Why didn't you tell me last night she was here?"

Don't get angry, he ordered himself. "Honey, you just got home ten minutes ago," he told her. "I haven't seen you since you went out last night."

"Would you have told me if the locket hadn't fallen out of your shirt?"

Her question took him back. "Of course I'd have told you," he said.

The pause. The words he knew were coming. *Don't,* he thought.

"Like you told me about Julia?" she asked quietly.

Even knowing that the words were coming, he felt stunned. "You're not trying to equate this with—?"

She wouldn't let him finish. "I'm trying to make our reconciliation work, David," she said. "What are *you* trying to do?"

He felt flabbergasted and angry at the same time. "What is going on here?" he asked. The numbness in his head aggravated him now, preventing clear thought.

"I think that's my question, David," Ellen said.

He stared at her, appalled. "You're not—?" He couldn't finish, kept staring at her. "You're not actually suggesting that—?" Again, he couldn't finish.

"Were you going to tell me, David?" she demanded.

"Yes, Ellen, *yes!"*

He felt immediate regret at having raised his voice. They looked at each other in heavy silence. David knew he had to speak, say something to end this terrible feeling.

"Look," he started. "I know you're still disturbed about what happened but this had no bearing whatever on—"

Her look of disbelief made him break off. He made an incredulous noise. "El, come *on,*" he said. "Do you really think I brought you all the way back here for a second honeymoon just to make out with some total stranger who—?" He broke off with a disgusted noise. And yet what she suspected wasn't inconceivable, his mind threw back, dismaying him.

Ellen's voice made him shudder as she said, "Julia was a total stranger to me, too."

"Oh, come on, Ellen. Please?"

"I have just gone through a year of lies and secrets, David. I'm a little weary of lies and secrets."

He was getting angry again. He started to nod. "You really think there's something going on here, don't you? You really think that while you were out walking, I took advantage of the time to—" He broke off, exasperated. "For pete's sake, Ellen!"

He watched her in amazement as she reached forward, dropped the locket into his shirt pocket and turned toward the staircase. *"Ellen,"* he said.

He looked at the staircase until he heard the bedroom door close upstairs. Abruptly, then, he started forward. "No," he muttered. "We're not going to let things go again. We're not."

He moved determinedly for the stairs, trying to think of some way he could reassure her. Instead, he found himself envisioning the ineffective creature he'd make trying to settle their difficulties while standing before her in bare feet. He faltered in mid-stride, considering the hasty donning of his socks and shoes. No. He shook his head and kept on moving. There was no time for that.

He started up the stairs two at a time, then jarred to a gasping halt as the studio door was opened and Marianna stood before him. David gaped at her, his heartbeat staggering.

"What's the matter?" she asked.

He swallowed hard. "You startled me," he said. He could barely speak.

"I'm sorry. I didn't mean to."

David looked at her, confused. "How long have you been here?" he asked.

"Just a little while," she said. "I came to see you but you weren't in the house. Then I heard you come in with your wife and—" she smiled, embarrassedly. "I was afraid she wouldn't understand so I . . . hid in here."

"Oh," he nodded, vaguely. Good God, had she heard everything that had gone on below? The idea made him cringe.

"Could I speak to you a minute?" she asked.

David glanced up the staircase worriedly.

"Just for a minute," Marianna said.

"Well . . . all right." His smile was awkward. "You want to come downstairs or—?"

"In here is fine."

David hesitated for a moment, then nodded once. "All right." He entered the studio as Marianna stepped aside, tensing a little as she closed the door. The room was as dark as it had been the night before; without moonlight, perhaps even darker. "Did you close the drapes?" he asked.

"I was afraid your wife might look in and see me if I didn't."

David grunted, nodding. He shifted his feet on the icy floorboards.

"Why are they bare?" Marianna asked.

"I got my shoes and socks wet."

"Why don't you sit on the couch? We can cover them with the blanket."

"Well—" He drew in restless breath. I have to see my wife, he thought. This is ridiculous.

"Come along," she said. He tightened as she took him by the hand and led him across the studio to the couch; despite his disenchantment with her, her closeness still affected him strongly.

"Sit," she said.

David sat down. He lifted up his right foot and wrapped both hands around it. "Good Lord, it's frozen," he said.

"Lift both of them," she told him.

Obediently, David shifted back and raised his legs, resting both feet on the couch. Marianna picked up the blanket and shook it open, David averting his face from the scale of dust. Spreading the blanket across his feet, Marianna tucked the edges in around his calves and ankles. "There," she said. She sat beside him.

David tried not to let her see or hear him swallow as

she gazed at him. Now that his eyes were becoming accustomed to the dark, he could see that it was not complete, enough light filtering through the drapes to dilute the blackness. Marianna was dressed the same, her skirt and sweater dimly lactescent in the gloom. Only her feet were different, shod in light sandals now.

Well? he thought, abruptly, *What do you want?* Somehow he couldn't bring himself to speak the words aloud. "I tried to bring back your locket," he said impulsively.

Marianna fingered idly at her throat. "That's right; I left it with you, didn't I?" she said.

He nodded slightly, wondering if she was going to say anything about her lie. When she didn't, he reached into his shirt pocket with brusque annoyance and drew out the chain and locket. "Here," he said.

"Thank you, David." That smile again; he fought against its effect, shivering as their fingers brushed together. Well, what do you want? he thought again. Again, he couldn't ask aloud.

"I—"

"What, David?"

He tensed. Nothing, he thought. Then, as she looked at him with curiosity, he added, uncomfortably, "I saw the photograph inside and I don't look a bit like your—Terry."

"I never said you did."

David frowned, perplexed, then realized that she hadn't. "Well, you—said I remind you of him," he muttered.

"You do," she told him. "Very much."

He flexed his teeth together. Somehow the conversation was proceeding as if he'd requested to see her rather than the opposite. He braced himself to ask her what it was she wanted. He had to get upstairs to Ellen.

"Here," she said. He started as she held out her hand. Gingerly, he took hold of the slender chain, his fingers twitching as the locket fell from her palm, causing it to jump reboundingly against his wrist. Marianna inclined her head and, reaching backward, gathered up her long, black hair, baring the nape of her neck. "Put it on me, please?" she asked. David tightened irritably, then seeing no way out of it, pinched a chain end between each thumb and index finger, stretched it taut and carried it across her head, lowering it past her face. The locket caught on Marianna's chin and, with a fragile sough of amusement, she raised her head briefly so that the locket dropped before her breasts, swinging in tiny, penduluming circles. David leaned in closer, trying, unsuccessfully, to join the links.

"What's the matter?" Marianna asked.

"I can't see what I'm doing."

Marianna pressed against him. "Here." He felt a silken tingling in the flesh as she rested her cheek against his drawn-up leg; now the back of her neck was only inches from his face, milk-white even in the gloom. He squinted, trying to see the opening in the catch. The ambrosial scent of her hair and skin began affecting him. It seemed as if his lips were being, irresistibly, attracted to her neck.

"How do you get in the house?" he asked, trying to prevent himself from kissing the neck.

"With a key."

"Of course." He closed his eyes, teeth clenching lightly. This is not the time for kissing unfamiliar

napes, he told himself. He opened his eyes. "I'm sorry;
I just can't see," he told her, giving up. "If we could
open the drapes a little . . ."

Marianna reached back and took the chain ends
from him. "There," she said, drawing away her hands
almost immediately. Why did you ask me to do it then?
he thought.

"Why did you tell me you live down the beach?" he
demanded.

"I do."

"Where? I saw only one house and that's locked
up."

"That's the wrong one then." Her voice was teasing.

"Where's the right one then?"

"Down the beach."

He tensed. "Around the bluff?"

"Mmm-hmm." She smiled. "You'll find it, David."

He shivered at the implication of her words. "Will
I?" he resisted.

"You're angry with me, aren't you?" Marianna laid
a hand on his and looked into his eyes.

David had the feeling that his answer should indi-
cate that he didn't know her well enough to feel any
such extreme emotion at her behavior. Instead, he felt
himself draw breath in, strainingly, and murmur,
"No."

Marianna's smile was radiant. "Good," she said, "I
don't want you ever to be angry with me."

Ever? he thought. What did that mean? He almost
asked, then caught himself.

"You like this room?" she asked.

"I . . . guess." She had him, constantly, off-balance,
it seemed.

"I love it," she said, "ever since that first night." He

felt her fingers tightening on his. "I met Terry on the beach," she told him. "I was taking a walk and he was standing by the water, looking out. We talked a while; then he invited me to his house for a drink. We sat up here and had some wine and talked. Later on, we made love. Right on this couch."

David started unexpectedly.

"Are you angry that I told you?" Marianna asked.

He swallowed, tried to smile. "No, it's . . . not my—"

"Yes, you are." She leaned against him, her expression saddening. "Don't be angry with me, David."

"I'm not," he said. There was a feeling in his stomach which he wasn't able to identify. Could it, possibly, be jealousy? The thought offended him. I really have to go, Marianna, he thought. He braced himself to tell her so.

"Darling, aren't you going to put your arm around me?" she asked.

Something burst inside him—like a globe of ice exploding. He realized, with a start, that it was fear and drove it off, affronted. He was acting like a nervous boy. Just because she'd asked—

The thought broke off as he watched his arm settling over Marianna's shoulders. No, wait, I didn't mean—! He tried to countermand the movement but it was done now; Marianna leaned against him with a sigh. She pressed her cheek to his shoulder, looking up at him. *Dear God, how beautiful she was.* He tried to think of Ellen crying in the bedroom, needing him, but the thought had no cohesion, breaking up and dissipating in the moment of its birth. There was only Marianna, dark eyes holding his, her lips so close that, if he were to lean forward just a little bit—

No, wait a minute, he thought.

"Please," she begged.

No. He tried to reason with himself—to no avail. The onward movement of his arm was halting, like the gesture of a marionette, imperfectly manipulated. *No,* he thought again, but the counsel of his mind was powerless to stop him. Marianna's face drew closer to him, drifting upward palely. Oh, now, wait a minute— Now her eyes were closing slowly, now the heated perfume of her breath was misting across his lower face. For God's sake, wait! Now her lips were touching his, their softness yielding to him. No! Now they pressed in harder, animated and demanding; now he felt the fingers of her right hand sliding deep into his hair to pull him closer yet. The shadows spun around him, holding him, together with her, in a warmly fragrant chrysalis of desire from which he was incapable of breaking loose.

When she let him go, he hitched up slightly, breathing hard. "Marianna, this is—"

"Love me, David."

Something hovered in his mind: decision, like an uncommitted bird, prepared to wheel away in flight or plummet downward in attack. He watched her look of undisguised want as she turned and rose to one knee, facing him. "Love me, David," she repeated, her voice commanding. No! he thought.

With an impotent shudder, David slid both arms around her and she fell against him, lips, hungrily, at his again. He pulled her violently to himself, the pressure of her jutting breasts arousing him still further. Suddenly, Marianna jerked his right arm free and, twisting slightly to the side, lifted his hand to her left breast. David cupped his palm across the thrusting cone and started fondling and massaging it, feeling, through the sweater, how its nipple hardened at his touch. Marianna licked his lips tempestuously. She raked her teeth across his cheek, her breath like spilling fire on his skin. "Anything!" she whispered in his ear.

Drawing back, eyes never leaving his, she tugged the sweater up across her head and slung it aside; David tightened at the prominence of her bust as she turned her back to him. "Quickly, darling." His fingers trembled as he picked the four hooks from their eyes. The brassiere ends sprang apart and Marianna shucked it into his lap. "Hands," she muttered. David held them out, numb and shaking, and she clutched them to the pendant arching of her breasts, hissing through her teeth, eyes hooded, as he dug his fingers into them. "More," she said. Gasping, David dropped his head and started kissing them. He ran his tongue across the large, stiffened nipples and she pulled him savagely against herself, a frenzied moaning in her throat. "Feed," she said. Her back went rigid as he began to suckle her. "Bite me, hurt me." Her hands were clutching at his head like talons of steel. "Take them," she ordered. "They're yours, *yours!*"

David felt himself the captive of a wild, erotic dream. How their clothes came off he couldn't tell. All he knew was that, magically, both of them were naked and Marianna was bestowing on him the kind of headlong wantonness that he'd imagined only in his most covert of fancies—wordless, unconfined, increasingly berserk, her exquisite face gone bestial with demented sensuality, her hands and mouth like swarming creatures on his flesh, her ivory body twisting, turning, offering every possible variety of sensation, driving him deeper and deeper into a pit of mind—consuming lust until, reared up on him, back arched and stiff, tumid breasts upthrust, her expression one of insensate abandonment, she drained his loins with such a violence that it seemed as if his very blood were pouring into her.

Then it was done and he was lying on his back in dead-weight torpor, looking up at her with eyes glazed by satiety. Still straddling him, Marianna leaned down and ran her moist tongue over his lips. "Did you like that?" she murmured.

He couldn't speak.

Marianna smiled. "I think you did," she said. "I think you loved it." She straightened, drawing in a breath that swelled her heavy, ovate breasts. "Again?" she asked.

He stared at her, incredulous. *"Now?"* he asked.

Marianna laughed indulgently. "No, I guess you need a little rest," she said.

"Don't you?"

Her smile hardened into one of carnal invitation. "I never need rest," she said.

David groaned a little. "You're a better man than I am—so to speak." He tried to will away the rising chill of guilt.

Marianna rose and stood beside the couch, gazing down at him. "Am I beautiful?" she asked.

"You're the most beautiful woman I've ever seen in my life."

"And do you love me?"

David looked up blankly. Love?

"Never mind. You will." Kneeling suddenly, she kissed him with possessive ardor, right hand clutching at his hair. "You're mine," she whispered, fiercely. *"Mine."*

David watched in apprehensive silence as she stood again and began to dress. Abruptly, it occurred to him that Ellen might have walked in on them at any time; that she might walk in on them now. His worried gaze flicked upward automatically.

"She didn't hear," Marianna told him.

David started. "How do you—?"

"I know," she broke in. Was she smiling? He couldn't tell; her face was lost in shadow. "And you don't have to worry." She picked up her brassiere and slipped it on. "You like my body?" she asked, reaching back to fasten it.

"Yes." He wasn't certain what his feeling was at that specific moment, his diffident anxiety for her to leave balanced by a fear of not seeing her again—both emotions complicated by a constantly enlarging guilt and a sense of irritation with her for assuming that his one concern was to avoid detection by his wife. He wished that he could sit up and speak to her accordingly—but he felt as if his limbs were coated with lead. He watched her movements as she dressed. In seconds, she was done and sitting by his side.

"I'm glad you like it," she told him, "because it's yours." Bending over, she kissed him lingeringly, her left hand caressing his body; David writhed at her touch, thinking, almost frightenedly: Don't!

Finally, she sat up. "You won't tell her, will you?" she said.

David tensed. Was it just imagination or had there really been a shade more bidding than appeal in Marianna's voice?

"Please don't," she said. "It would ruin everything." She stroked his cheek. "And you *do* want me again, don't you?" She leaned down quickly and touched her lips to his. "Please?"

"All right." He felt incapable of saying no to her.

"Thank you, darling." Marianna stood. "You won't be sorry." A grating harshness thickened her voice as she said, "I'll give you everything you've ever wanted. Everything."

David started as, without another word, she turned and headed for the door. "Wait," he muttered. It took all his strength to push up on an elbow. Before he could speak again, she'd gone into the hall and shut the door behind herself. Would Ellen hear? he thought, grimacing. Would she hear the footsteps on the stairs? He listened tensely for the sound of the front door closing but it didn't come. At least, she'd done that soundlessly. He wondered if, despite what she'd said, Marianna *wanted* Ellen to know.

Abruptly, David shivered. It was freezing in the studio—as though, with her departure, Marianna had removed all warmth. As quickly as he could, he struggled to his feet and started dressing, skin speckled by gooseflesh. By the time he'd finished, his legs could barely support him and he sank down with an enervated groan, fumbling for the blanket, lifting it infirmly and drawing it around his quivering back and shoulders. God, but he was cold!—and tired. He winced in dismayed confusion. And thirsty too; his throat felt blotted dry. He had to have a drink of water—and yet he wondered if he had the strength even to stand much less to cross the studio, exit and climb the staircase to the bedroom. And if he were able to manage all that, how could he face Ellen?

He shook his head, trying to smile but knowing that the smile was forced; his sense of humor had all but deserted him, it seemed. Well, how could it be otherwise? He'd just committed brutally heedless adultery and it wasn't very funny. No matter how advanced one's taste for drollery might be, there were circumstances which could not, possibly, be construed as comical. Perhaps his sense of fun wasn't worldly enough—because he just couldn't see any humor in the situation.

He shook his head despondently. Don't think about it, he told himself; get a drink and go to bed. He raised the iron bar which was his left arm and looked at his watch. Twenty minutes to two. He'd been here less than half an hour. It was inconceivable. For all he remembered of it, a century might have gone by in that time. Straining to his feet, the blanket slipping to the floor, David dressed and hobbled palsiedly across the room. Liza crossing the ice, he thought. That didn't amuse him either.

He thought he'd never reach the door. By the time his hand had clutched the frigid knob, his legs were vibrating beneath the cumbrance of his body, threatening to give way at any moment. David leaned hard against the door, breathing with effort. Dear God, was he going to make it? This was practically ridiculous. What had she done to him? He'd never felt so washed out in his life. Was this what sex of such ferocity did to a man? He felt a formless harrying of resentment that he didn't really know, not with Ellen, not with Julia. Still, this weariness did seem inordinately extreme.

"The hell—" he muttered. Clenching teeth, he jerked opened the door and stumbled into the hall, shutting the door behind himself. He hesitated for a moment, then turned upward, fearful that he might lose balance if he tried descending. Besides, something drew him toward Ellen; an insistent need which he could not recognize. All he knew was that it had nothing to do with guilt.

The first step up left him aghast. He might have been a statue trying to ascend the upstairs. *What had she done to him?* The realization that less than thirty minutes with her had reduced him to a state of near collapse angered as much as stunned him. Good Christ, I'm forty-six, not eighty-six! he thought.

Determined not to sit, he lumbered up the remaining steps, moving with a tight-lipped persistence until he'd reached the landing. There, he permitted himself to rest—but, as a wave of dizziness began oppressing him, he staggered into the icebox gloom of the bathroom and threw cold water on his face. This gave him the strength to fill the glass five times and drink; gratefully, he felt the moisture penetrating his system, laving parched tissue.

Ellen was lying on the unmade bed, the comforter over her. Her back was turned to the door and she seemed to be asleep. She must be exhausted too, David thought as he shuffled across the floor. He sank down on the bed, trying not to groan but unable to restrain it. God in Heaven; he felt as if his flesh and bones were melting, oozing down into the mattress. It took every bit of power he could summon to raise his legs. He fell back on the pillow with a lifeless thud.

Almost immediately, he began to shiver. He should have crawled beneath the comforter with her, he realized. Now it was too late; he knew he didn't have the energy to move again. His teeth started to chatter and he tried to stop them, finding it impossible. He felt his body vibrate with convulsive, uncontrollable shivers.

He had never been so cold in his life. Despite that, he could feel himself receding into dark oblivion.

He managed to raise his deadened eyelids as Ellen turned. She was looking at him strangely. "What's the matter?" she asked. He couldn't speak. Ellen leaned in closer, her expression vague, unreadable. "Are you sick?" she asked.

He thought he shook his head. His body jolted as a violent shudder wracked it.

"You're shaking so."

"I know. I'm . . ." He swallowed and it made a dry sticking sound in his throat.

Ellen looked at him several moments more as if trying to assess what had brought him to this state. Now he was able to interpret her expression as she sidetracked anger and resentment for concern. "Here, can you move?" she asked.

"Uh?"

"I'll put the comforter on you."

He couldn't move; Ellen had to tug the comforter loose. She spread it over him, the weight of it making him shiver even more. "What *is* it?" Ellen asked.

He shook his head feebly, a murmur stirring in his throat. Ellen stared at him in mute disquiet, then, impulsively, pulled the comforter back across herself and shifted to his side. She pressed against him and he felt her right hand touch his chest. "You're so *cold*," she said. She looked suddenly distraught. "Oh, David, I'm sorry, I didn't know you were this upset." A withering pang of guilt stabbed through him as he realized that she thought he was this way because of what had happened between them.

"Darling; you're shivering so hard." Ellen slid her

arm around him and snuggled closer still. She hadn't put her blouse back on and the feeling of the bust against him made him colder yet, reminding him of the sick derangement with which he'd rioted in the heavy succulence of Marianna's breasts. He closed his eyes, shuddering as he bit into his lower lip. I'm sorry, Ellen, he thought. I'm sorry; please forgive me.

"Shh, darling. It's all right," she whispered and he realized, with a start, that he must have spoken the words aloud; he hadn't been aware of it. He'd have to watch himself to make sure he didn't, inadvertently, tell her what had happened. Conscience always finds its voice, he thought as he pressed his face against her shoulder. Despite everything, he was grateful for her warmth and comfort. He held on to her with almost desperation, thinking: She wouldn't stay like this if she knew what happened. Then his brain was sucked down rapidly into a little death of sleep.

He thought he'd dozed an hour or so. Opening his eyes, he looked, with groggy dullness, at the window. It was dark outside. For several vacuous moments, he tried to guess the cause of darkness in the day time. Storm? Fog? Eclipse? His sluggish mind could not decide. Then, suddenly, awareness came and, wincing, he thought: Good Christ, it's night time. He raised his hand and lower arm and read the watch face; it was almost seven. He let his hand drop heavily to the bed.

"Awake?"

Starting, David looked around. Ellen was seated at the lamp-lit dressing table, legs crossed, fastening her stocking to a garter strap. He stared at her in puzzlement. Beneath the open robe she wore her black merry widow. He watched in stolid curiosity as she leaned forward to pull on black, high-heeled shoes. Where was she going? He hadn't seen her in the merry widow for years; she didn't like to wear it because it was so binding. For a moment he had the unsettling notion that she'd given up on him and had a date. But with whom?

Ellen straightened up and glanced at his reflection in the mirror. "Sleep good?" she asked. He saw that she was smiling and returned it, sheepishly.

"I guess I did," he answered. "I didn't mean to sleep so long. I just . . ." He shrugged, not knowing what to say.

"You needed this vacation," Ellen told him. "You've been at it harder than you think."

"I guess." He nodded. Observing, suddenly, that, in addition to everything else, her hair had been set, he felt a tremor of uneasiness. Swallowing, he asked, "Got a date?" He tried to sound amused.

"Mmm-hmm." She was brushing her hair now and the silken, crackling noise made David shiver.

"I realize that the poor sap of a husband is always last to know," he said, "but, uh—" He cleared his throat. "—Am I acquainted with the bastard?"

Ellen nodded. "He's a famous television writer."

A rush of grateful pleasure seemed to warm him. David grinned. By God, he really *had* believed there might be someone else. "Whose initials are?" he asked.

"D. C."

"David Copperfield?"

"Cooper."

David grunted in disdain. "The King of the Sack Outs, you mean,"

Ellen repressed a smile. "He's pretty nice when he's awake," she said.

David sat up. "Where's he taking you?" he asked.

"Oh—" She gestured airily and he noticed, with fresh surprise, that her nails were painted, too; she hadn't done that in years. She looked strikingly trim and luxuriant sitting there, her waist drawn in, hips full and rounded, breasts molded tautly, long legs sheathed in dark silk, face made up with care. "I don't know," she finished. "Dinner and dancing, I think. Something like that."

"He may expect reimbursement," David warned her. "You know what those Hollywood men are like."

Ellen looked across her shoulder at him. "Reimbursement?" Her expression was adroitly credulous.

"As they say," he answered, "in coin of the realm."

She pursed her lips as though in estimation, smiled politely. "Fair exchange," she said.

"The price is right?"

She nodded and stood. Don't let me fail her now, he thought. As she turned to let him look at her, he wondered why he feared that he might.

"Approved?" she asked.

"You look marvelous." He ran his gaze across her figure. "We may never get to dinner," he added, uncomfortably aware of exaggerating her effect on him.

"Yes, we will," she said. "You have to play the game."

"Drat," he murmured.

"Do I really look all right?" she asked, concerned.

"Like a billion dollars. In gold."

"Really, David."

"Honey, you look wonderful."

Ellen sighed. "I'm so glad," she said. "I want to look nice for you."

David stood and moved across the room, burdened

by remorseful guilt. He took her in his arms and held her close. He pressed his lips against her neck and closed his eyes, the fragrance of her perfumed skin filling his nostrils. "You smell ambrosial," he murmured.

"Is that good?"

He bit her gently on the shoulder and straightened up, a tongue-in-cheek expression on his face. "Ain't bad," he said.

Her smile was soft with love. "I'm glad," she said. "I want to please you."

"Oh—" He squeezed her so hard that she gasped. "You're good," he said. "So good."

She clucked as though in disappointment. "And here I thought I looked so wicked."

"You do." He kissed the tip of her nose. "You look as wicked as hell. You are Thais, Jezebel, and Messalina rolled into one."

"Don't forget Clara Bow."

"Noted." David smiled at her. "And now it's time I made *myself* bewitching. Or, as we phrased it in the last campaign—excluding one word for the sake of delicacy—shave, shower, shampoo and shoe-shine. *If* you'll excuse me—" He started across the room.

A few moments later, he closed the bathroom door and leaned his back against it wearily. Please, don't let me hurt her, he thought again. He closed his eyes, face a mask of apprehension. Why was he so afraid? He didn't know, yet it was there, oppressively there. Pushing from the door, he stepped over to the window. It was too dark for him to see the Sound but he could hear, as always, the muffled booming of its surf. Somewhere, out there, is Marianna, he thought.

Not all of her though; the recognition came with stunning force. Part of her she'd left behind.

He could feel it, living, in his flesh.

As David turned the car to the left, Ellen let the movement press her to his side. David took his right hand from the steering wheel and squeezed her leg. She leaned over to rest her head on his shoulder. "It's been a nice night," he said, pleased when she responded, "Wonderful."

It *had* been wonderful. After phoning Linda to find out that everything was fine and the baby wasn't born yet, they'd driven across the Island to Bay Shore to discover, with relief, that the seafood restaurant they remembered from their honeymoon was still in operation. There, they'd ordered the same meal they had enjoyed then—cocktails, cups of creamy clam chowder, a shared Caesar salad, then boullibaise, coffee and dessert. There had even been the same white wine with which they'd toasted one another again, clinking glasses together and smiling at each other across the dim-lit table.

Away from the house and reminders of Marianna, in this location associated with their happier past, David had begun to feel a diminishing of that vague, impenetrable fear; a resurgance of hope. Marianna wasn't going to return; and he'd already realized that, because they loved each other, there was no reason at all why he and Ellen could not resolve their difficulty. He'd relaxed after that, the restful atmosphere plus the martinis and wine contributing further to his sense of well-being. At least five times during the meal he had thought: I'll make it up to her.

After dinner, they'd gone for a drive toward the middle of the Island and found a roadhouse with a trio that played for dancing. They'd stayed there several hours, having a few drinks and circling slowly around the near empty dance floor, enjoying each other's warmth and closeness.

"I'm glad you thought of this," he told her.

"So am I."

David nodded. "Good." As he spoke, he felt a wave of vague depression settling over him. Oh, Christ, not again he almost said aloud. He felt like suggesting that they not go back to the house. Away from it, Marianna had, for all her fascination, assumed her realistic place in his life which, compared to Ellen's, was insignificant. He didn't want that to change and had a sudden inclination to turn the car and head directly for the airport, get them home as soon as possible, back to the things they knew and understood. They hadn't brought along so many possessions that they couldn't afford the loss of them. True, it was an extravagant notion, but one that seemed extremely desirable to him.

"Deep thoughts?" Ellen asked.

David glanced over with a hurried smile. "Not very deep," he said.

"You seemed far away."

He squeezed her leg again. "Just relaxed," he told her, "I was right beside you all the time."

"Good." She kissed his cheek. "That's where I want you."

As the car moved slowly along the half block which constituted the business section of Logan Beach, David saw lights in the drug store. "Care for some ice cream?" he asked.

Ellen seemed to mull it over. Yes, David prompted

her mentally, wanting to delay, at least for minutes more, their return to the house. He felt his grip begin to tighten on the steering wheel, then slacken as she answered, in a pleased voice, "Why not?" Angling the car, he parked in front of the post office and they both got out. A black, immaculately cared for Bentley stood nearby. David eyed its glossy elegance with admiration. "Beautiful," he said. He took her arm and walked her toward the drug store.

The counter was to their left as they entered. At its further end, the owner of the store was talking with a well-dressed woman in her sixties. Both looked over as the door was opened and the woman smiled. "Good evening," she said.

"Evenin', folks," the owner greeted.

They smiled back, nodding. "Good evening." Settling on adjoining stools, they waited while the owner came to serve them.

"Help you?"

David glanced at Ellen. "Honey?"

"Oh . . . let's see." She wrinkled her nose a little. "I think hot chocolate," she decided.

"Make it two," David said.

"Okeedoke." The man moved away and David looked at Ellen.

"It's a little cold for ice cream," she said, linking her arm to his.

David leaned over and kissed her cheek. As he straightened up, he saw that the woman was still looking at them. She smiled and he noticed how attractive she was for her age, well-groomed and almost statuesque; she reminded him of some actress.

"I'm sorry," she said. "I didn't mean to stare. It's just

that we rarely have visitors this time of year." Her gaze shifted to Ellen. "You aren't local people, are you?"

Ellen smiled back at her. "No; we're from Los Angeles."

"Los Angeles." The woman looked impressed. "You *are* far from home. Surely you didn't come all this distance just to visit Logan Beach."

"Well, you see, we spent our honeymoon here and—"

"Ah." The woman smiled and nodded. "And you've come back to see it again."

"That's right."

"Does it look much different to you?"

"No; I don't—think so." Ellen didn't sound too certain. "About the same."

"Except that our honeymoon cottage was blown to sea by a hurricane," David added.

"Oh, dear." The woman clucked in sympathy. "How terrible. You wanted to stay in it, of course."

"We found a nice place, though," Ellen said.

"Oh; I'm glad. In Logan Beach?"

"Yes." Ellen nodded. "Right by the water. It's a lovely spot."

The woman glanced at David. "By the bluff?" she asked.

"Yes."

"I thought I saw lights down there," she said. It *was* her, on the bluff he thought. Why had he been so certain? "Is that your house up on top?" he asked.

"Yes."

"We've admired it," Ellen said. "It's beautiful."

"Thank you." The woman bowed her head once.

"Perhaps you'll pay me a visit before you leave." She smiled. "My name is Grace Brentwood."

"Oh . . . yes," Ellen said. "I'm sorry; we haven't introduced ourselves. This is my husband, David Cooper. My name is Ellen."

"Delighted."

"Pleased to meet you," David murmured. He tried not to but all he could think of was that Mrs. Brentwood probably knew Marianna; knew about her, at least.

"This is Mr. Doty," Mrs. Brentwood told them, gesturing toward the owner of the store. The man smiled as he put their cups of hot chocolate on the counter.

"Glad to meet you folks," he said. They smiled back.

"Well, I'm so pleased that we ran into each other this way," Mrs. Brentwood said. "Although, we might have met on the beach."

"You go there often?" David asked.

"All the time. I love to walk there."

She *must* know Marianna then, David thought.

He nodded, wondering what question he could, safely, ask. After a few moments, he thought of something. "When I was out walking yesterday morning—" he began.

"That *was* you I saw then." Mrs. Brentwood interrupted

"Yes." David smiled. "Anyway I ran across a closed-up cottage down the beach. Is that yours, too?"

"Yes. It was used as a beach house once; but it's been closed for years. There's only me now and I'm afraid my swimming days are over."

"You live alone?" asked Ellen.

"Except for the servants," Mrs. Brentwood said.

David considered asking whether there were any

other houses nearby, deciding that he'd better not. He had no reason to ask at any rate, he thought, self-critically. Marianna was no longer a part of his life.

"You know who owns the cottage we're staying in?" he asked.

"Someone from the city, I believe." Mrs. Brentwood said. "I've never met them." She smiled. "So are you enjoying your holiday so far?"

"Yes. Very much," he said.

"The cottage was cold until the gas was turned on but it's very comfortable now," Ellen added.

"Good. I hope you find your stay there pleasant."

"Thank you."

"How long do you expect to be there?"

"Until next Thursday, probably."

"I see."

David took a sip of hot chocolate and put down his cup. "Does anyone live there any more?" he asked.

"Not on a regular basis, no."

"It's just rented in the summer?"

Mrs. Brentwood shrugged a little. "I suppose."

Who was there last summer? The question flared across his mind. "How old a place is it?" he asked.

"I don't remember really," Mrs. Brentwood answered. "It seems as though it was built when I was just a little girl though."

David cleared his throat. "Painter live there once?" he asked.

"Painter?"

"An artist." David felt his heartbeat quickening as though he'd blundered somehow. "We were looking at his paintings in the cottage," he said. "Or hers," he added; not too quickly, he hoped.

Mrs. Brentwood nodded, smiling. "I really have no

idea," she said. "I don't pay much attention to who stays in the cottage; I'm sorry."

Forcing a smile, David turned away and drank some more hot chocolate. For some reason he had the rattled feeling that he'd given himself away even though he was certain that he hadn't. Good old guilt, he thought in disgust. He listened with half an ear as Ellen said, "We were admiring the paintings."

Mrs. Brentwood looked at her lapel watch. "Oh, dear," she said. "Way past my bedtime." She drained her cup of tea and stood.

David rose from his stool as Mrs. Brentwood stopped in front of them and extended her hand to Ellen. "Do come and see me now," she said, smiling.

"We will," Ellen told her.

"Good." Mrs. Brentwood held out her hand to David and he took hold of it; her grip was cool and firm. She gazed fixedly into his eyes and, suddenly, he felt his stomach cramping. Good God, was it possible that she'd seen Marianna going in and out of the cottage? For an appalling instant, he imagined her up on the bluff, peering downward through binoculars, keeping watch on him. What if she did know Marianna? What if Marianna had a reputation for this sort of thing? A wave of dread broke over him. Mrs. Brentwood seemed benevolent enough; but what if she was only waiting for a chance to talk to Ellen, tell her what she knew? He swallowed hard, barely hearing as she said, "Good night, Mr. Cooper," and headed for the doorway.

Lethargically, he settled on the stool again, noting Mrs. Brentwood's exit from the corners of his eyes. I'm just no good at this, he thought gloomily; deception under fire was definitely not his forte. How he'd managed it with Julia he couldn't imagine now. He felt

like blurting everything to Ellen, then recognized that
he was seeking the easy way out; confession, absolu-
tion.

As the door closed, Ellen said, "Good-looking
woman."

"Yeah."

"She must have been beautiful when she was
young. Even now she's attractive and she must be
more than sixty."

"Mmm."

"Don't you think so?"

He shook his mind loose. "What, that she's attractive or more than sixty?"

"Both."

"Yes and yes." He managed a smile.

"I think she liked you."

David tightened. "Me?"

"The way she looked at you," Ellen teased.

"I'm very attractive to old ladies," he said.

Ellen made an amused sound and, suddenly, an
overwhelming urge swept over him again; to drive, at
once, to the airport and go home. More and more, he
had this harrowing, inchoate dread that something
terrible was going to happen if they didn't leave. He
could see no reasonable logic behind it; the episode
with Marianna was concluded and it certainly
stretched credulity to believe that Mrs. Brentwood had
been spying on him and intended to betray him. Still,
he was unable to shake off this fear. If it is only guilt,
it was the worst case he had suffered in his life.

"Honey?"

David started. "Mmm?"

"I said, I think the man wants to close up."

"Oh?" He looked around and saw that Mr. Doty had

his overcoat and hat on and was emptying the contents of the cash register into a paper sack. "What makes you think he wants to close up?" he asked.

They paid for the hot chocolates, said goodnight and left the drug store. Breath clouding from their lips, they linked arms and hurried to the car. "Cold," she said.

"That's a fact," he answered. Hastily he pulled open the car door on the driver's side and Ellen scuttled in. She pressed against him, shivering, as he dropped beside her and pulled the door shut.

"Oooh," she muttered in a shaking voice. "My hot chocolate's turning into milkshake."

David smiled and switched on the motor, pushing the heater control to *High.* Looking across his shoulder, he backed out into the street, braked, then started forward.

"Think we ought to visit her?" she asked.

"If there's time," he said. How would Ellen react if he were to suggest going home tonight? he wondered. Was there anything he could say to disguise the fact that it would be no more nor less than abject flight? He couldn't tell her about Marianna, couldn't mention his uneasiness regarding Mrs. Brentwood. Ellen would think that their attempted second honeymoon was a failure in his eyes; that he wanted to escape it. Above all, she mustn't think that; not now.

Ellen groaned a little. "Oh; this merry widow," she said.

"Hurt your stomach?"

"They ought to call it The Iron Maiden."

"Take it off."

"Well—" She hesitated for a moment. "I know how you like it."

David swallowed, realizing that she meant it always excited him to make love to her while she wore it. He felt a stirring in his flesh which was both desire and anxiety; he mustn't fail her again. "I do," he said, "but I don't want you to have a stomachache."

Again she hesitated. "You're sure you don't mind?"

He caressed her leg. "Not as long as I can watch," he said.

"Fresh." She removed his hand. "We haven't even met."

"Sure we have," he said. Opening her coat, he put his hand on her leg again and tugged her skirt and slip up past her knees, heartened by the gratifying reflex in his body. "Allow me to assist you in the shedding of your garment," he said.

"That's mighty white of you."

"I aims to please." He pulled her skirt up further, uncovering her stocking tops and the white flesh of her thighs. "Oo-la-la," he muttered, croakingly.

"I guess it's warm enough now," she said.

"Vous said it." David watched with sidelong glances as she removed her coat and threw it on the back seat. Unbuttoning her dress, she started to unzip the front of her merry widow. "Oh," he said, his tone aggrieved.

"What's up?"

"Me, almost."

"Why the groan then?"

"Well," he said. "I presumed that everything was coming off."

She slapped his shoulder lightly. "What are you saying?"

"Quelle funzies, madame."

Ellen grunted in mock indignation, then sighed concedingly. "Oh, well," she said. "Franco-American relations, I suppose." She worked her dress and slip up past her waist, then pulled them over her head and lay them on top of her coat. She started to undo the garter strap from her stockings when David stopped her.

"Uh-uh," he said.

She gazed at him loweringly. "Have you been snowing me?" she asked.

Reaching forward, David twisted the light control knob, turning on the overhead bulb. Ellen started. "David."

"That's my name."

She glanced around uneasily, then, seeing only darkness everywhere, settled back and crossed her legs. "All right," she said, "let's just hope there isn't a gendarme lurking behind some tree."

David didn't answer, looking at her. He could feel desire mounting in him. If only he could lose himself this instant, drive away all apprehensions.

"Le chat got your tongue?" she asked.

"You will soon find out who has my tongue, madame."

"Don't you think you'd better douse the—?" she began, then broke off as he turned the light off. He pushed the knob in, cutting off the outside lights as well, guided the car off the road. Braking it on the shoulder, he twisted the key to the left, stopping the motor but leaving the heater on.

"Yes?" she asked, suspiciously.

He turned to her, breath already quickening. With hurried movements, he discarded his suit coat and sweater; Ellen watched as he threw them in back. "Here?" she asked, trying to sound amused but only half succeeding.

"Why not?" Twisting around, he put his hands on

her. She made no sound as he pushed her head back with a kiss, running his hand across the taut projection of her breasts. He wanted her now. It wouldn't be the same at the house.

Ellen was pressed against his mouth now, her full lips parting under his. Their tongues began to play and David drew her upward, pulling her around until she straddled his lap. She was making tiny, whimpering noises which, he sensed, were as much worried as stimulated. He couldn't stop, though; here, he could satisfy her, here it would work. He rubbed her back with slow caresses, then, reaching in between their bodies, found the zipper tab and pulled it down. He cupped his hands around her heated breasts, fondling and squeezing as they kissed. Ellen pulled her head back, breathing hard. "Oh God, I want to, darling, but—" She broke off, gasping, as he forced her back against the steering wheel, held apart the bone-stiff edges of her merry widow and, leaning forward, began to kiss her breasts and suckle them. *"David,"* she said, almost sobbing. She grabbed at his shoulders with talon-hard fingers, then, teeth clenching, seized her breasts and held them tautly to his lips.

Suddenly she threw herself against him with a startled gasp and, jerking up his head, David saw the headlights of an approaching car. Blinded by the glare, he ducked his head back down, eyes closing. "Oh, Christ," he muttered.

Ellen veered away from him and pulled her legs free; half crouching on the seat, she pulled at the zipper of her merry widow. "We'd better go," she said, unable to conceal her disconcertion.

"All right." He twisted the ignition key and gunned the starting motor. Switching on the lights, he thumbed the transmission bar to *Drive.* They were on the road before the other car went by.

For almost a minute, neither of them spoke. Then, as Ellen finished pulling on her top coat, David said, "I'm sorry, honey."

"That's all right." She shivered fitfully. "It's not your fault."

"Well, I—" David swallowed "—might have found us a better spot." If only he could tell her that it hadn't been just a propensity for the unconventional; that he'd been afraid he couldn't satisfy her at the house. "You *were* excited, weren't you?" he asked.

"I'm not impervious, David," she said, her soft laugh insufficient to hide the pique behind her words.

"I know that, honey. I just want to be sure you weren't pretending for my sake."

Ellen sighed. "I'm not that clever," she said.

David's grip contracted on the wheel rim. Damn it all, he thought; she'd been so beautifully excited, too. He felt the chill of sudden foreboding. What if that was all there was tonight? The idea made him queasy. "I'm sorry, El," he said. "I really am."

"There's nothing to be sorry about," she said. She drew her coat together. "I was getting kind of cold anyway."

You didn't feel cold, he thought. He let it go. "I'll start a nice, big fire in the living room," he said.

"Or in the bedroom."

No, he thought. That wouldn't do. Circumstances wouldn't be the same up there; in bed, they'd probably go to sleep. And he had to satisfy her tonight—he just had to. He wondered, briefly, if he dared suggest finding a more isolated place to park, then decided against it. This time, she would, surely, ask him why he didn't want to return to the house—and, beyond some vague excuse about not caring for its atmosphere, he had no answer. Anyway, he thought, there was no justifiable answer. The distraction was in him, not the house. Actually, he could make love to her there with far more ease; there was comfortable furniture, a fireplace, liquor, warmth and, most important, time and privacy.

Cheered by this, David turned left and started driving down the hill which led to the beach road. He glanced towards the house on the bluff and saw that all its lights were out; Mrs. Brentwood must have gone to bed as soon as she'd gotten home. The memory of her face cut fleetingly across his mind. Who was it she reminded him of? Gladys Cooper? Irene Dunne?

He glanced at Ellen. "Warmer now?"

"Fine."

No more was said before they reached the house. David kept thinking of things to say but decided, each time, that she would prefer not to talk, needing time to regain composure. He wanted very much for her to have regained it by the time he tried to make love to her at the house.

For that matter, he'd better start recovering himself, he realized. At the moment, sex seemed rather uninviting. It was incredible how rapidly desire could flare, then, with equal rapidity, disappear entirely. Under less demanding circumstances, he wouldn't even be considering an attempt to re-establish a romantic bond; being a writer had the advantage, at least, of making him sensitive to mood. As things were, however, he felt that he had no choice. He had not made truly satisfying love to Ellen in far too long a time and, except for the unpleasant incident several minutes ago, the events of the evening seemed natural forerunners to lovemaking; it would be a shame to dissipate the aura of warmth and intimacy which their hours together had generated. It had to be tonight. They'd started on the wrong foot, true, but it was still the logical time.

When they reached the house, he switched off the motor and put his arms around Ellen. He kissed her cheek, a corner of her lips. "I love you, El," he said.

She leaned her head against his and closed his eyes. "I love you, too," she murmured. She kissed his cheek. "It's been a lovely night."

"It isn't over yet."

"No." Her tone was noncommittal, making David realize that he would have to win back her interest. He wished that he didn't feel it was so important, but he did.

"Nobody can come driving through the living room," he told her.

Ellen made a faint noise but he wasn't certain if it was amusement or not. He reached beneath the coat and stroked his palm along her leg, making her flinch a little. "Madame is oblivious?" he asked, part edgy, part intimidated.

"Madame wants to warm her carcass first," she said.

"Done and done." He patted her leg. Inside, warmed by the fire, a few martinis in her, she'd be all right.

Ellen got her clothes and they ran to the front door, breath steaming. As he was trying to unlock the door, David dropped the ring of keys and couldn't find it for nearly a minute, during that time torn between the impulse to curse at the bad luck which was making Ellen even colder and the inclination to laugh at his impression of himself, planning seduction when he couldn't even get the front door open. He settled for the compromise of silence, found the key ring in the sand and opened the door. With a faint, tremulous moan, Ellen scuttled across the living room, dropped her clothes on a chair, and stood close to the gas heater, holding open her coat.

David shut the door and looked around, partially expecting to see Marianna in the room. A condensation of the resulting scene flickered through his mind: Ellen seeing her, finding out who she was, discovering her relationship to him. He shivered. *Good ol' guilt,* he thought. Striding across the rug, he set fire to some crumpled newspaper, then dumped in driftwood fragments until flames began to crackle noisily, popping sparks in all directions. Stepping back, he looked at the fire briefly, then turned to Ellen.

She was still by the heater, standing, legs apart, the coat held open. "Getting warmed up?" he asked. Her answer was a groan of pleasure.

"That, I take it, is assent," he said, heading toward the dining alcove. Pushing into the kitchen, he turned on the overhead light. He took a pair of glasses from the cabinet above the sink, got the bottle of martini mix out of the refrigerator and returned to the living room.

He glanced at Ellen as he poured her drink, pleased again to feel the molten pressure of desire in his loins. The skin of her thighs and upper chest appeared milk white against the blackness of her corselet and stockings. She looked little short of tantalizing with her arms outstretched, holding the coat wide open, her eyes shut and her lower trunk thrust forward toward the heater. "You make a dandy flasher," he said.

She smiled.

"Here we go." He held out the glass to her. Ellen opened her eyes and looked at it. "For me?" she asked. It sounded less a question than a mild dissent. David felt himself begin to tighten. "Warm you up," he said.

"Well . . ." She hesitated for another few seconds, then smiled. "All right." She took the glass and waited as he poured his own martini.

David put the bottle down on the table beside the heater and held up his drink. "To us?" he toasted.

Ellen raised her glass and clinked it against his. "To us."

They each took a swallow and Ellen grimaced. "I don't know if I'm ever going to get with martinis," she said.

David braced himself and worked his left arm around her waist beneath the coat. Leaning over, he kissed the warm flesh above her breasts, feeling, on the back of his neck, the buffeting heat from the gas flame. He straightened up and smiled at her. "You feel warm now," he said.

"Just about." She looked into his eyes as if in search of something.

"What?" he asked.

She swallowed, dropped her gaze, then finally raised it again. "You do love me, don't you?" she asked.

"Of course, I—"

"Think," she interrupted, her tone one of almost fright. "Before you answer, think about it."

He wasn't certain whether it was fear or determination which made him put down his drink, embrace and kiss her. At first, she only allowed him to do it, showing no reaction. Then, he felt her starting to respond and, taking the drink from her hand, he put it next to his own. Ellen slid her arms around his back and held him tightly as they kissed again. She drew her head back, breathing quickly. "*Do* you?" she demanded.

"Yes."

"Then say it."

David grasped at her hair with his left hand and kissed her hard. I do! he told himself. "I love you," he told her, startled at the husky quavering in his voice.

"Darling." Ellen dropped her arms and let the coat fall. "Love me," she whispered.

David kissed her lingeringly, then, turning from her, moved to the sofa and pushed it against the raised hearth. He threw more driftwood on the fire and hurried back to Ellen, leading her across the room. Without a word, she clambered onto the sofa, hissing at the coldness of the cushions. David got their drinks and, settling down beside her, handed her one of the glasses. "Drink," he said.

Obediently, she took a sip.

"All of it," he told her.

Ellen raised the glass and swallowed every drop, gasping as she finished. She looked at him a moment, then, abruptly, threw her glass into the fireplace. "You," she muttered. David drained his glass and slung it after hers.

Eyes never leaving his, Ellen rose to her knees and sat astride his lap again. "It's going to be the way it used to be," she said. "The way it used to be." Leaning back, she unzipped her merry widow all the way and pulled apart its hooks and eyes. Letting it flop behind her on the hearth, she cupped both hands beneath her breasts and held them up. "For you," she said. "With love."

David hugged her tightly, pressing his face against her chest. Now! he heard a voice commanding in his mind. He wanted desperately to lose himself in Ellen, forgetting everything except his love for her. "You're my life . . . my life," he murmured as he kissed her breasts.

"Darling." Ellen almost sobbed the word and, looking up, he saw a glistening of tears in her eyes. Shaking, he began to kiss her lips and cheeks. Don't let me fail her, please don't let me fail her! Unexpectedly, he groaned, unable to control it, shuddering as she took the groan for passion instead of what it was. Her fingers trembled, opening his clothes. Too much! he heard the voice again. He couldn't stay with her, couldn't match the rising frenzy of her need. Terror filled him. He began to shiver, breathing as convulsively as Ellen but with dread instead of ardor. His body felt distended, fevered, yet something held him, locked and helpless, allowing his desire to build but forbidding its expression—something deep within him, cold and poisonous, that had trapped his vitals and would not release them. Waves of nausea began assailing him. The room commenced to tilt and buckle. Ellen's face became a pallid gelatine before his eyes. *I'm sick*! he thought in sudden horror. This was madness, this was what it felt like when the mind collapsed. He waited for the screams to crowd his throat.

They never came. Abruptly, it was done and Ellen slumped against him, panting, eyes closed. Sight and balance flooded back across him and he found himself staring at the fire with the distinct impression that he hadn't seen it for a long while. The sensation of abrupt recovery from unconsciousness pervaded him. The last time he had felt this way was when he'd bobbed up out of darkness as the sodium pentothal, which an oral surgeon had administered, wore off. There was that same feeling of baffled dullness, of having been the victim of duplicity. Added to this was the chilling knowledge that, in terms of anything beyond the barest physical gratification, he had, as dreaded, failed her once again.

Ellen raised up slowly and looked at him. "You didn't, did you?" she said.

He swallowed. "Yes," he said. "A little bit; in the beginning. I couldn't hold it back."

"Oh."

"I'm sorry."

"That's all right."

He bent forward and kissed her gently. "I wish it could have been together," he said. He pressed his cheek to hers and closed his eyes. "It was wonderful," he told her. "It really was. Just like it used to be."

He didn't even try to pretend that she believed him.

David lay inertly on his back, staring up into the darkness. Ellen was asleep. He listened to her breathing, deep and slow. At least he'd given her the mitigation of physical relief, he thought. It wasn't much, but it was something. As for himself, the unexpended desire throbbed inside him still, waiting for release.

Why hadn't that release come before? he wondered again. Was their relationship at such an impasse that his body rebelled against it? There seemed no other feasible explanation. The circumstances had been extremely provocative—the fire's heat and flickering light, the amnesic mellowing of alcohol, Ellen's amorous appearance and behavior. What more could he want?

Marianna, said his mind.

He writhed a little, glowering. I have to sleep, he

thought. They'd gone to bed hours ago, yet here he was still wide awake. Either I can't keep my eyes open or I can't get them shut, he thought disgustedly. He twisted onto his right side and stared at the dormer window.

With increasing irritation, he listened to the dull explosions of surf in the distance. Why doesn't someone turn the damn thing off? he thought. He clenched his teeth and hissed out jaded breath. Where was Marianna now? He thrust aside the question, but it kept returning. He still didn't know where she lived. For a brief while, he had thought that she actually might live in that house on the bluff, but meeting Mrs. Brentwood had disposed of that idea. Where did she live then? What the hell's the difference? he demanded of himself. He tried to blank his mind. Sleep, he told himself; just sleep.

After a while, he sat up with a rumbling sigh. Ellen stirred, then slipped back into heavy sleep. Standing, he moved to the rocking chair and sat on its edge. What the hell am I doing this for? he wondered. Already, his feet were cold, the pajamas chilly on his skin. Why didn't he go back to bed and warm up?

Instead, he donned his bathrobe and slippers and sat on a window seat, looking out. Below, the ivory roof of the car glinted in the moonlight, reminding him how luminescent the studio floor must be in the same light.

What if Marianna were down there at this moment, waiting for him?

David shivered fitfully. They'd better go home in the morning; he was weakening again. He scowled. The hell I will, he thought; I'm staying right here.

What if she were down there? He couldn't rid himself of the notion. What would he do if he were to descend to the studio and find her? Would he be able to send her off again? The way he felt? He shuddered, thinking of her body, of the way in which she'd given it. A sudden wave of blind, unreasoning desire swept across him and he came upon himself standing up. Shuddering, he sat again, glaring through the window, fingers tapping on the seat. Come on, come on, he thought; in reference to what, he had no idea. He glanced across his shoulder at Ellen, somehow aggravated by her being so immersed in sleep.

All right, he thought, abruptly, she can do it, I can do it; he'd get dressed and walk. Shunning the implication that he had in mind, determining where Marianna lived, he stood and moved to the rocking chair, unfastening his bathrobe. He pulled his clothes on hastily, making no attempt at stealth, part of him, he sensed, wanting Ellen to wake up and talk him out of it.

She didn't wake up. She didn't even stir. Dressed in under a minute, David walked to the bed and stood beside it, looking down at her. It was too dark for him to see her face; she was a shadow, a sound. I don't really want to go, he told her in his mind. For some reason he felt afraid. Turning quickly, he left the room. He'd get his camping jacket now, leave the house and walk along the beach. To where? goaded his mind. He ignored it.

As he reached the landing, an impulse struck him to enter the studio and, opening the door, he went inside. Unable to see a thing, he felt his way across the floor and pulled a drape aside. Déjà vu! he thought. The instant seemed a startling duplication of the one the night before when he had stood here looking at the moon-silvered beach, the frothy breaking of the waves.

As he recalled, the beauty of it had depressed him then as well. The only difference seemed to be that he was going out to walk instead of Ellen.

When the door clicked shut, it was as though he dropped, abruptly, into icy water. He whirled, the jolting of his heartbeat like a fist blow at his chest.

"I'm back," she said.

He stared at the outline of her, motionless beyond the reach of moonlight.

"I've been here all night," she told him, "waiting for you."

"Here?" His voice was barely audible.

"I tried to stay away. I couldn't though. I came back and used my key."

He swallowed, trying to regain control. "How long ago?" he asked.

"It doesn't matter now," she said. He watched uneasily as she moved across the studio, tightening when, without a moment's hesitation, she pressed against him, sliding her arms around his back. He felt the magnetic drawing again. "You want me, don't you?" she murmured. It was not a question.

The studio seemed strangely warm, the air heavy with a kind of musky, clinging redolence. "You're mine now, aren't you?" she said.

"I—"

"Aren't you?"

David shook his head, unable to speak. As he watched in mute distraction, Marianna stepped back, smiling, and with languid grace, crossed her arms at the waist and pulled her sweater up. He trembled as she dropped it on the floor and started to remove her skirt. He stared at her in torpid silence, knowing that he couldn't leave. Marianna knew it, too. Her movements were prolonged as she unhooked her bra, then, leaning forward slowly, let it flutter loose. She straightened up and stood erect before him, pale, voluptuous, her incredible beauty bathed in moonlight. David murmured, "God."

Marianna thrust her arms out and he lurched to her embrace, their bodies clinging as they kissed with savage fervor. Marianna's lips spread open under his, her head twisting from side to side. Suddenly, she bit his neck. "Mine!" she gasped.

"Yes."

"Say it, then!"

"Yours." His voice went grating, maddened. "Yours!"

A piercing coldness wrenched up violently in his stomach, making him cry out in shock. Suddenly weak, he clung to Marianna, gasping. "What—?" he mumbled.

"Darling, darling."

"What?"

"You're mine now. Mine."

"What was it?" He was almost pleading.

Smiling, Marianna drew him to the couch.

"Our wedding," she said.

SATURDAY

Ellen put down the news section of the *New York Times* and looked across the room at him; he had, just now, halted on the bottom step. "Well," she said. It was almost two o'clock.

In the momentary silence, challenge seemed to flash between them. "I'm sorry I slept so late," he said. He tried to sound crisp and unperturbed but only sounded tired.

"Don't be silly," Ellen told him. "That's what we're here for."

Is it? David nearly asked. He nodded once and headed for the kitchen painfully aware that his gait was close to that of an old man.

Ellen began to put aside the newspaper section. "Don't get up," he told her.

"I don't mind."

"I'm only having coffee," he explained.

"You aren't hungry?"

"No." The thought of eating was repellant to him. "I'll have some breakfast later."

"Brunch," she said.

"Or brupper." He was startled by the rancor in his

voice and, stopping, looked at her with an affected smile. "Where'd you get the paper?" he asked.

"In town."

"You've been to town?"

"I had a lot of time," she said.

Was she baiting him deliberately? He turned toward the kitchen again. Crossing the dining alcove, he pushed open the door.

It was cold in the kitchen. David shivered as he poured some coffee into a pan and began to heat it. He thought about having a slice of buttered toast but even that seemed offensive. His stomach was oppressively on edge, the start of a headache pulsing at his skull. He got a drink of water from the sink; his fourth since waking up. It's like a hangover, he thought; except that one martini could scarcely be the cause. His drunkenness had been with Marianna's flesh. The memory of that lunatic intoxication made him shudder.

He focused his eyes to see the coffee boiling. Turning off the flame, he poured it into a mug and set the pan in the sink. The involuntary groan he uttered, sitting down, made him wince. He leaned back heavily against the chair, his body feeling ponderous. He'd slept for nearly twelve hours, too; close to half a day, for Christ's sake. David shook his head, grimacing. He was coming apart at the seams. Another day or so, I'll be a basket case, he thought.

He wrapped his chilled fingers around the mug. He ought to sit in the other room; it was warm there. He didn't budge. He had the odd conviction that he'd taken root. He sighed and took a sip of coffee. Even raising his arm felt strenuous. He looked at the mug as he set it down. It was like the ones Ellen and he had used when they were first married. As he recalled, they'd cost a quarter apiece in those days.

He shivered convulsively. God, this place is cold! he thought. He still couldn't fathom how the unheated studio could feel so warm when he and Marianna were together. Granted, I'm in flames, he thought, derisively; still—

The thought broke off as Ellen pushed into the kitchen. "Why are you sitting here?" she asked. "It's cold."

"I know."

He must have looked and sounded pitiful, he realized. Ellen's smile was almost pained. She lay her hand on his shoulder and squeezed it once. "Sit in the dining room," she said.

"All right." He tried to stand without revealing his fatigue.

"That's all you're having?" Ellen asked.

"Yes."

"I'll be glad to make you some bacon and eggs."

"No, no, this is fine. I haven't really woken up yet." I mean my appetite hasn't woken up yet, he thought defensively. He considered saying it aloud. "Join me," he said, appalled by the weariness in his voice.

Ellen hesitated. "Well—" She looked around. "Is there any coffee left?"

"I think so."

David watched her lift the pot and shake it. As she moved to get the pan, he turned away. "I'll wait outside," he said. She didn't answer.

He sat in one of the captain's chairs, his back to the window. I should have gotten dressed, he thought. It would have made his being up seem more official. He stared at his hands holding the mug. The low-ceilinged alcove was dim and shadowy. He glanced across his shoulder, frowning. Another scintillating day, he thought. He turned back, blowing out disgruntled breath.

He gazed at his hands again, wondering where Marianna was. Still in bed, sleeping off last night's dissipation? He closed his eyes. He simply could not believe it, that was all. He knew it had happened, yet it seemed, like last time, more the memory of a lurid dream than of reality. And it wasn't only guilt-afflicted conscience looking for a subterfuge. What had occurred was, literally, unbelievable. Marianna was a paradox. She came and went without consistency. Physically, he knew her, yes; knew her with such brutish incontinence that, even now, the memory of it choked his breath. Beyond that, there was nothing. He blinked, incredulous, realizing that he didn't even know her last name. When she'd introduced herself, it had seemed quixotically fitting that she tell him only her first name. Now, suddenly, it seemed preposterous. One name, no address, almost no identity. It made him feel obtuse, insensitive.

He glanced aside as Ellen came in, carrying a mug of coffee. "Would you like some cookies?" she asked.

"No, thank you."

She sat across from him and they exchanged polite smiles. "Did you sleep all right?" she asked.

"Yes; thank you."

No, thank you. Yes, thank you. David thought: Any moment now, we'll start addressing each other as Mr. and Mrs. Cooper. He started feebly. "What?"

"Did *you*?" she repeated.

"Uh . . . not too well." He'd been about to answer

that he'd slept like a block of wood but decided that she'd wonder then why he was still so tired.

"I'm sorry," Ellen said. "Were you sick?"

"A little bit. Wine with dinner always gets to me."

She nodded, then in several moments said, "If you don't feel well—"

"What?"

"Go back to bed."

He would have taken prompt advantage of her suggestions if it hadn't made him bristle so. "I'll be all right," he said. What would you like to do today? he heared himself inquiring in his mind. We could take that picnic. He didn't choose to repeat the words aloud. He had no wish to go on a picnic or even to find out what she'd like to do. He wanted to go back to bed and sleep some more. He wanted Marianna to join him in bed and—

"What's the matter?" Ellen asked as he shivered.

"What?"

"You have a chill?"

"It's cold in here." He took a sip of coffee. "I'll get dressed," he said. He rubbed at his forehead, grimacing.

"What's the matter?" she asked again.

He squinted at her. "What?"

"You have a headache, too?" Her tone was formal.

"A little bit," he answered stiffly.

"Maybe you're coming down with something."

"Maybe."

"You've always been susceptible to flu."

"Have I?" He knew how hostile he sounded but didn't care.

Ellen's smile was distant. "Haven't you?" The truth of her words only plagued him further.

"This conversation doesn't seem to be going any-where," he said.

"I'm sorry."

David drew in a pacifying breath, released it shak-ingly. "Been up long?" he asked, saying the first thing that occurred to him.

"Since eight," she said.

That's six long hours, isn't it? he heard his mind retort. He nodded, then began to yawn before he could control it.

"Still tired?" she asked.

"No, I'm not still tired."

Her expression was unreadable. "You yawned," she said.

"True." His smile was fleeting. "I do that every now and then."

"So I've noticed." Ellen gazed into her coffee with a bleak expression.

David breathed in deeply. He couldn't seem to get enough air in his lungs. He frowned, realizing that he wanted another drink of water.

"David, what is wrong?" she asked.

"*Nothing.*" He shifted on the chair, feeling trapped and restless. "Ellen, I just got up." Her expression made him irritable. "All right, it's this cottage," he said. "We should get away from it."

"What difference does the location make?" she de-manded. "The trouble is with us."

He felt a burst of fear inside himself. "It's not," he said. "It's this cottage."

Ellen shook her head. "It's not the cottage and you know it," she told him. "It's our marriage." She lowered her head. "What's left of it," she murmured. Her hands were clasping on the table now, the fingers rigid, white.

He felt his muscles tightening. "Do I have to spend the rest of my life in a state of penitence?" he asked.

Ellen looked up in defiance. "Would you feel the same if it was me who'd had the affair instead of you?"

A sense of unreality made David's head feel numb. He knew that she was talking about Julia but, horribly, it all fit what had happened with Marianna as well. "It was not an affair," he said. "I thought I wanted to marry her."

"Why didn't you then?" She was brushing away tears as if infuriated by the weakness which had caused them.

"Do we have to go through that again!" he asked, trying not to let himself be angry. "Do I have to say it again? All right. I will. I didn't want to lose what you and I have together."

"Which is—?" she asked in a faltering voice.

"A lot, Ellen. If you'd—"

She wouldn't let him finish. "Call it what you like," she said. "It was an affair."

"No, it wasn't," he snapped. "Our marriage was falling apart when I met—"

Again, she interrupted. "Why was it falling apart? *Why*?"

"What difference does that make now?"

"I want to hear!"

"You know the reasons as well as I do. Too many hours at work. Two small children. Lack of time together. Your background, my background. What's the difference?"

"That's really facing it," she said, her voice grown hard.

"Facing what?" he demanded.

"The fact that we are almost strangers."

"Oh; I see." He felt barely able to speak. "I guess I've been wrong in thinking we had something all these years."

"Oh!" She jolted with incensed frustration, then controlled herself. "Of course, we had something," she said, severely. "Would we have stayed together twenty-one years if there hadn't been something? But there wasn't enough. We never went below the surface. Now that surface is wearing thin and there's nothing underneath to hold us up. The heart isn't there, David; it just isn't there. I'm going to be a grandmother. A *grand*mother, David. I'm not even sure I know what it is to be a wife."

David felt as though he'd been mysteriously transposed, replacing the man who was supposed to be sitting here, listening to these words. All he could reflect on was that Ellen minded being a grandmother. He knew that it was just a fragment of the truth but it was all he could grasp at the moment.

"You know what I feel like?" she asked. She gazed at him accusingly. "Like a betrayed wife. A second time."

He was already shocked. This new blow only made his stomach muscles cramp a little more.

"I know it isn't true," she said. "It's just the way I feel. Because the kind of secrecy you used to hide your affair from me is the kind you've always used to hide yourself from me. I don't know you, David. Not what's down inside. You're kind and gentle and—fun to be with but—I just don't know you. Maybe that goes both ways; I suppose it does. Maybe I'm as secretive as you are. I don't mean to be, don't want to be but maybe I am—and maybe it's because you never gave me the chance to tell you what I really feel. Maybe I've held it back because I knew you didn't want to hear it.

"We've never discussed things, David! Never! Not the really important things—what we are, what we believe about ourselves, about our marriage. Our relationship has been like a—an iceberg. The part that's been exposed is just a tiny part. Most of it is still submerged. We've talked and we've talked but we've never really said anything, never probed or searched. We haven't built a relationship, we've avoided one. We've been pretending with our married life instead of living it." Her voice began to break. "I know it's hideous for me to say this to you after twenty-one years. It makes me sick to say it—me, forty-two, you, forty-six. And here, for the first time, I'm saying it. *The first time, David.*"

The stillness following was so oppressively heavy that he imagined he could feel it weighing on him. His body seemed to be carved from massive, fragile glass; he knew that it would shatter if he moved. The room appeared askew, about to tilt. Any second now, his chair would topple and he'd fall, splintering into a thousand fragments. Ellen, help me. Somewhere in the deadened hollow of his mind, a voice was pleading.

Ellen closed her eyes abruptly, pressing out tears that trickled down her cheeks. She wiped them off. "I'm sorry," she said. "I apologize. It wasn't very nice of me to hit you like this when you've just woken up." She inhaled deeply, tremulously. "I didn't intend to do it," she added. "I didn't mean for it to end like this."

David nodded, murmuring, "I understand." He didn't. He felt totally disoriented, cut loose from his moorings, his mind adrift in eddies of confusion. The only thought he could retain, because it chilled him so, was that, without actually knowing about Marianna, Ellen had, somehow, sensed her existence.

The rest of it he was unable to cope with. It was too vast, too all-encompassing. How could one begin to reappraise a relationship of twenty-one years?

The alcove and the house seemed deathly still. The only sound was the remote, incessant boom of waves striking the shore. Both of them sat mutely, frozen in their separate isolations. Nothing more to say, David's mind repeated several times. He knew it wasn't so, that just the opposite was true. There was so much to talk about, it was impossible to find a starting point. Things had gone too far.

"Well," he said. His voice was quiet, passive. "Under the circumstances, it doesn't make much sense to ask what you want to do today. Or tomorrow or . . ." His voice trailed off, he leaned back tiredly against the chair. Three thousand miles they'd traveled to renew their waning marriage, he thought, and, in a matter of days, it had collapsed entirely. He swallowed, feeling cold and ill. It seemed impossible. Then again, perhaps it had been inevitable. Perhaps Marianna had only hastened what was bound to happen anyway.

He looked up, twitching, as Ellen rose and started for the living room. "I'm going for a walk," she said.

He nodded, even though he knew she couldn't see him. He watched as she picked up her camping jacket from a chair and pulled it on. She started for the front door, then stopped to look at him, her face expressionless, the pain apparent only in her eyes.

"I put it all too harshly, I'm afraid," she said. "It's not as if we haven't had a good life together. Or that you haven't been a good husband. It's just that . . . well, we're getting older now. The children have their own lives; it's only you and me. There should be something in our marriage to sustain us—something to carry us through these difficult years." She shook her head. "I just don't think there is," she said, unhappily. "I think there'll be another Julia." She hurried to the door and left.

David sat immobile, feeling paralyzed. She's leaving me, he thought. He listened for the sound of the engine, then realized that the ignition key was in his trousers pocket upstairs. Where was she going then? For a walk, she'd said. But he couldn't believe that she was coming back.

He blanked his mind deliberately and stood, observing his movements as he might those of someone else while he pushed open the kitchen door, crossed to the sink and filled a glass with water. Drinking, he caught sight of Ellen through the window. She was walking along the beach in the opposite direction from the bluff. He watched her move farther and farther away, her figure shrinking imperceptibly until it was a length which he could span between a thumb and index finger. At that point, he turned away.

Moving into the living room, he sat on the sofa and picked up the bulk of the *Times*, depositing it on his lap. Ellen had moved the sofa back to its original position. He couldn't seem to recollect how it had been to push it up against the hearth and make love to her on it. Those moments seemed so long ago. It was bewildering to think that it happened only last night. Since they'd come to Logan Beach, time had become grotesquely attenuated. The moment of their arrival seemed the distant past and life in Sherman Oaks had all the aspects of an ill-remembered dream.

David sighed and turned the first page of the news section, looking down sightlessly at the print. Never discussed anything? he thought. How could she say that? They'd talked about their families, the children, his work and aspirations, hers, life in general; so many things, he couldn't possibly enumerate them. None of which went far below the surface though, the thought assailed.

David shuddered. For a moment he felt terrified and lost. Then the fear was ended; he was conscious only of desire for Marianna. Why not? he thought. Was he to spend the rest of his life in unresolved despair with Ellen? "To hell with that!" he muttered, slapping fiercely at the pile of newspaper sections, scattering them in all directions.

Again, he shuddered, staring at the disarray of pages on the floor. What was wrong with him? He shook his head as if recovering from a blow. Guilt again, he thought. He nodded vengefully. By God, he was sick and tired of guilt. He recalled the icy wrenching of it in his stomach last night when he'd told Marianna that he was hers. Why shouldn't he have told her? Why shouldn't he be hers? Even though she'd told him, afterward, that she was only teasing about their "wedding," why shouldn't there be one?

Lurching to his feet, he started for the stairs. He'd dress, find out where Marianna lived, tell her that he—

David jerked around as someone knocked on the door. Marianna! he thought. But why should she be knocking? All the other times she'd come right in.

Maybe the door was locked and she'd forgotten her key, he guessed as he moved across the living room. Had she been waiting down the beach, seen Ellen leaving? David reached the door and found that it *was* locked. He twisted the latch knob and pulled it open.

Mrs. Brentwood returned his smile. "Good afternoon."

"Good afternoon." He stared at her. She was wearing a tweed skirt and suede jacket belted at the waist, a white, silk scarf around her neck. Her cheeks were reddened by the wind.

"How are you?" she asked.

"Fine." His tone was undetermined. Taking her extended hand, he shook it once.

"May I come in?"

David started. "Yes, of course. I'm sorry, I wasn't thinking." He stepped to the side. "Please; come in." He caught the scent of her perfume as she entered. Closing the door, he turned to face her, dreading that she'd come to tell him how she'd noticed Marianna entering and leaving. "My wife's not here right now," he told her.

"I know," she said. "I saw her leaving."

David forced a smile. Now he was certain that she'd come to speak of Marianna. "She should be back soon," he said.

Without replying, Mrs. Brentwood looked around the room as though in search of something. David felt himself starting to bristle. Did she think he'd hidden Marianna in a closet or behind a chair?"

"You want to sit—?" he started to say.

"Here is fine" she said. She smiled at him. "Well," she continued, "how do you like it here?"

David held himself in check. Even if she did know something, he wasn't going to let her trick him into verifying it. "Fine," he answered. "It's very pleasant."

"Yes." She nodded, looking around again. A war of

nerves? he thought. He forced himself to smile as she returned her gaze. "I didn't ask last night," she said. "It didn't seem appropriate; but have you seen its ghost yet?"

David's smile went faintly quizzical. "Its what?" he asked. He was sure he hadn't heard correctly.

"Its ghost."

He blinked. "I thought that's what you said."

"You haven't seen it then?"

David gestured toward the living room, surprised to notice that his hand was trembling. "Here?" he asked.

She didn't answer, looking at him warily. At last, she nodded. "Here," she said.

He wanted to swallow, but felt that he should not permit himself such a telltale reaction. "Well," he said, "that's fascinating." He wondered why he felt so ill-at-ease about it. "You should have told us last night."

"I didn't want your wife to know," she said.

He felt his stomach muscles quivering. "Why?"

Again she failed to answer, eyes unblinking, fixed on him; they frightened him somehow. "Whose ghost?" he heard himself ask.

"You believe it then?"

He laughed awkwardly. "Well," he said. He gestured as though embarrassed. "I hardly know you well enough to say that you're making it up."

Mrs. Brentwood's eyes remained on his. "The ghost is that of a young woman," she said.

David stared at her without expression.

"Don't you want to know her name?" she asked.

It's Marianna, isn't it? he thought, startled at his prompt acceptance of the idea. "What?" he asked.

"Marianna."

"Oh." He nodded, two things suddenly established

in his mind: One, that ghosts did not exist; two, that he had no intention of revealing anything to Mrs. Brentwood. Strengthened by the double certainty, he said, "That's a pretty name."

"You've never heard it before?"

"Well, not in reference to—"

"And you haven't seen her."

"Mrs. Brentwood—" David gestured, smiling with polite dubiety. "No; I haven't." His smile grew teasing. "Are you disappointed?"

"Yes, I am," she said. "In you."

He tensed involuntarily. "I'm afraid I don't understand that."

"You don't."

"I don't." His tone verged on animosity. "Perhaps you'll explain."

Her smile, though hinting at derision, seemed sincere enough to be disarming. "No," she said, "there's nothing to explain. If you haven't seen her, you haven't seen her." She looked around again, then back at him. "Be glad you haven't," she continued. "You would find it most unpleasant if you did."

"Why, is she ugly?" That was better; bland, aloof.

Mrs. Brentwood looked amused. "Ugly?" she repeated. "Hardly. She's the most beautiful woman I've ever seen."

"You've seen her then." He tried to sound intrigued.

Her gaze read his with curious detachment. "How else could I have known about her?" she asked.

"I gathered from what you said last night that you knew very little about the cottage." David's tone was openly challenging now.

Mrs. Brentwood smiled. "I know enough," she said.

David tried to look disinterested.

"I see her as I walk," she told him. "She watches me."

Something aberrant in her tone made David look more closely at her, sensing that he'd found a key. "From where?" he asked.

"The studio."

He nodded. "And are you the only one who's seen her?"

Mrs. Brentwood's smile was one of cool detachment. "Mr. Cooper, I have lived for sixty-seven years," she said. "I have yet to have my first hallucination."

David tightened. "You have no doubts, then, that this—this—"

"Marianna," she supplied, her tone implying that she knew he was aware of the name.

"Yes," he said. "You know that she's a ghost."

Her answer was another smile.

"All right," he said, concedingly. "I'll be predictable and ask. How do you know?"

"For the very simple reason, Mr. Cooper, that she died some years ago."

David was unable to prevent himself from shuddering.

"You look distressed," she said.

"Well—" He managed a straining smile. "It isn't every day that . . ." He wanted her to leave and yet he couldn't let her go; he had to hear it all now. "Were you a witness to her death?" he asked.

"I·saw her afterward," she answered. David waited, staring at her. "Her corpse, that is," she said.

He shivered violently.

"You *have* seen her, haven't you?" Mrs. Brentwood said.

"What?" he frowned. "I told you—"

"I know what you've told me," she cut him off. "I, also, know what I see."

"See?" His effort to sound merely curious was unsuccessful.

"Your face," she said. He stiffened as she put her hand on his arm. "Leave the house, Mr. Cooper," she said.

"What do you mean about my face?"

She drew her hand away with a sigh. "Very well, then, we'll assume that you have not seen Marianna," she began.

"Mrs. Brentwood—!"

"All right; you haven't seen her then." She ran her gaze across his face. "Unfortunately, whether you have or not, you've been exposed to her. And suffered by her presence."

Abruptly, he felt stripped of logic and defense. "Which means?" he asked.

"Which means that there is terrible depletion in your face," she said. "The depletion which is brought about by psychic attack."

David struggled back toward rationality. "I'm afraid that sounds absurd," he said.

"You're exhausted, aren't you?" she told him. "You sleep too much. You have a dreadful thirst which cannot be relieved. Your solar plexus feels abused and tender. Please—don't bother to deny it. I'm not here to argue, only to persuade you to quit this house."

Mrs. Brentwood's words had acted on him like a surgeon's scalpel, slicing away the last of his assurance. That she knew these things appalled him. He still fought against accepting the idea of ghosts—a

subject which had always evoked skeptical amusement in him—but he could no longer avoid a chilling
infestation of fear.

"Will you go?" she asked. "There's no need to tell
your wife if that concerns you. Give her some other
reason for leaving."

Despite his unsettled state, David felt the lancing of
a cruel amusement. Getting Ellen to leave was hardly
the greatest of his problems right now.

"There's a small inn several miles along the beach,"
Mrs. Brentwood said. "Very charming, very clean. I
know the manager; I'll phone him if you like. I do suggest you go there though." Her gaze probed sharply
into his. "Immediately."

David looked at her in silence.

"You will find," she said, "that shortly after you
have left, a sense of peace will come to you."

"I see," was all he could reply.

"I hope you do, Mr. Cooper. I'm sure you pride yourself on being an intelligent man. I'm sure you are accustomed to demanding facts. Don't let that habit
blind your insight. As illogical as it all sounds to you,
let your intuition have its way—for it believes me if
your mind does not. Later on is time enough for delving
into facts." Her fingers gripped his arm again. "Only
one thing matters now," she said. "That you leave this
house."

David swallowed dryly. "Am I the first you've said
this to?" he asked, still searching for an answer.

"By no means," she answered. "Without going into
details, I've done everything I could, in past years, to
keep this house untenanted. I've made myself a dreadful bother, I'm afraid—but in a good cause, Mr.
Cooper."

"I thought you paid no attention to who stayed in the—"

"Mr. Cooper," she interrupted. "That was last night. This is now. *Listen* to me. Because of my efforts, there hasn't been more than a handful of people here in many years—and only one of those was—"

"What?" he asked when it became clear that she didn't mean to continue.

"I don't—" Mrs. Brentwood braced herself. "No," she said, "You ought to know. It was a young man who lived here one summer. Against my advice, he remained in the house for nearly four months.

"And?"

"He had to be removed by force. He was committed to a mental institution."

David felt the pulsing of a vein in his right temple.

"I believe that he fell victim to Marianna's influence," she said, "and was possessed by her."

He tensed. "Possessed?"

"Taken over," she explained. "His mind controlled by hers."

David clenched his teeth. It isn't true, he told himself. He wouldn't buy it. When he was alone, he'd work it out.

"Marianna, you see, is what is known as an earthbound spirit," Mrs. Brentwood told him. "Probably the most insidious psychic force to which man is subject. Because, while not alive themselves, the earthbound choose to dwell among the living, seeking to control and use them. They reject the hereafter, wanting to believe—indeed, in most cases, actually believing— that they are still alive, that nothing has been changed."

"How do you know all this?" he asked.

"Having finally accepted Marianna's existence," she answered, "—and I assure you that it took me just as long as it will take you—I made it my business to know. In order to protect those who might chance to stay in this house."

"Why should you want to protect them?"

Her smile was almost sorrowful. "Why does any human being want to protect another?" she asked.

"Sorry," he said, not certain whether he was or not.

Mrs. Brentwood looked around, grimacing slightly. "I must go now," she said. "I dislike being in this house." She forced a smile. "Goodbye, Mr. Cooper. After you've gone to the inn, come and visit me."

David's first impression as the door thumped shut was one of dazed awakening. He closed his eyes, then opened them. Had Mrs. Brentwood really been here? Had she really said the things that filled his mind? Unreality crowded in around him; he didn't know which way to turn. It was not enough to disparage. Not when confirming evidence seemed to flood across him.

The way he'd met Marianna. The way she always came to him—without a sign, appearing suddenly. The outfit she wore, always the same; a summer outfit in the winter. Bare feet; sandals. When he went out, it was in heavy clothes and shoes. If she really came along the beach, how could she keep warm in such inadequate attire? Which raised the point that he had never seen her outside, never found that so-called "house down the beach."

And why were they always in darkness or in semi-darkness? The only time he'd seen her in anything approaching daylight had been yesterday when she'd appeared by the front door; and, immediately after-ward—at her insistence—they had gone up to the studio, to the darkness. That strange sensation in his stomach. His unnatural lassitude. What had Mrs. Brentwood called it? Psychic depletion? That ghastly wrenching in his stomach last night! *Our wedding.*

"Oh, my God," he muttered in sudden, terrified revulsion.

With his shudder came reaction. "Bull!" he snapped. He was behaving like a credulous fool. There could be any number of legitimate explanations. Mrs. Brentwood had been so damned melodramatic that she'd thrown him totally off-balance, then kept him there; he hadn't used his brain once. It was her eyes, he decided. Well, those eyes were gone now—and the contradictions were appearing.

A ghost with a warm-fleshed body? A ghost a man could make love to? A ghost with clothes, required to remove those clothes by undressing? A ghost that owned a locket and chain he could keep in his pocket overnight? Did she walk through walls, evaporate? She did not. She used doors like anyone else. She walked on stairs with very audible footsteps. She *breathed,* for Christ's sake!

David make a sound of disgust. How quickly Mrs. Brentwood had deluded him; why she wanted to, he didn't know. He also didn't know how she'd discovered he was tired and thirsty, that his stomach muscles hurt. He was sure that there were explanations, though. Perhaps she'd guessed. No, that was unlikely. Facts then. She'd observed that he almost never left the house. She'd seen the way he walked, the way he looked, and had concluded, logically enough, that he was tired. She'd seen Marianna entering and leaving. From this, it was obvious deduction that his stomach muscles would be aching, that he'd be tired and thirsty. Especially if Marianna had a reputation for this sort of thing.

And speaking of facts, he thought, abruptly, Mrs. Brentwood had been precious sparing with them. Without going into details, she'd said. That seemed to be the gist of her approach. All she'd really told him was that Marianna was the ghost of a young woman who had died some years ago. What year? How?—and why? Who was the young man who had supposedly gone insane here? When had it happened? Where had he been committed? Was he still there? Why should only men be subject to Marianna's will? What had Mrs. Brentwood done to keep this house untenanted? Spoken to the realtor? The owner? Tried to have it condemned?

Not one of these facts had she tendered—not a date, a name, a reason. She'd given him, instead, high drama and mysterioso. He had no idea why she'd done this or what the truth really was—except that it did not include Marianna's being a ghost. All he was certain of was that Mrs. Brentwood had lied to him. Why hadn't he been aware of it at the time? God knew, he'd been exposed enough to that sort of thing on television and in grade-B movies. He should be immune by now. Why wasn't he?

The answer was a simple one, of course. It was not sequential to apply, to life, the critical values one exercised in judging dramaturgy. Had he witnessed Mrs. Brentwood's performance on a screen, he would have grasped its flaws immediately. As it was, she'd stood before him in the flesh—a real woman speaking real words. At least he had assumed the words to be real.

What else could he have assumed? How often, in his life, had he met anyone who lied so well that the feeling of consistent truth was imparted? The last such person he recalled was a boy he'd known in high school who had lied about his female conquests with incredible skill. He'd been fooled then and he'd been fooled now; only the length of his gullibility had differed. Not that he felt particularly stupid because of this. It was only common sense to function on the premise that people told the truth when they spoke. This was not the sign of a pollyanna attitude, merely a reasonable—and fundamentally workable—assumption.

An assumption which failed only when one came across a person like Mrs. Brentwood. He knew, especially now, what it was too create, by omission—subjects avoided, issues skirted—an atmosphere of partial deception. But never had he created a structure of deliberate lies in order to victimize Ellen or anyone else; nor was he capable of truly understanding anyone doing such a thing to him. That Mrs. Brentwood might, conceivably, believe what she'd told him only made the problem more disturbing than ever. To all appearances, she was as sane as he. Certainly a passing strangeness in the eyes, an occasional betraying tremor in the voice was not enough to translate into aberration.

Still, it was simpler to accept that than the notion of ghosts. That, he refused to acknowledge; it offended and defied every logic he believed in. He could readjust his mind to encompass the probability of Mrs. Brentwood's alienation but not to admit the concept of life beyond death. If only there were some facts on which to build this mental readjustment; something tangible to serve as cornerstone. A single fact.

As if in answer, David found his gaze attracted toward the painting hung above the fireplace mantel. *Painting,* he thought. Abruptly, he snapped his fingers, turned and ran to the steps, ascending two at a time. There *was* a fact he could establish!

Entering the studio, he moved along the east wall, looking for the outline of a door, the parted drapes admitted enough light for him to see. After several minutes, he found the parallel cracks and ran his fingers up and down the right-hand one as Marianna had done. Locating the catch, he pressed it and the door sprang ajar. He pulled it open and went inside. As he entered, he grimaced at the smell, a fusion of dust, mold and dampness. He hadn't been bothered by it Thursday night; astonishing what rhapsodical distraction could do.

Breathing through his mouth, he walked to the painting and pulled it over to a patch of dim light. Disappointment made him frown. The portrait was nowhere near as fascinating this time. Not that it was unattractive; but he could see, now, that the artist had completely failed to capture Marianna's beauty.

He rubbed a fingertip across its surface. It was coated with a film of greyish dust. Looking closer, he was able to make out a network of infinitesimal cracks in the paint. Even assuming extreme dampness and dust accumulation, it was difficult to see how any painting could age so radically in a period of months. Swallowing, he rubbed away the dust on its lower right-hand corner. The letters T. L. were exposed, beneath them a numbered date. David leaned in closer, squinting. 7-10—He rubbed at the canvas, then, abruptly, jerked his hand back with a harrowed gasp.

The final number was 37.

"David?"

He gasped again, twisting around so sharply that he almost fell. Crouched in darkness, he gaped at Marianna's silhouette in the doorway, a wave of chilling, primitive dread plunging across him. His limbs felt frozen, locked; he couldn't think.

"I had to wait until she'd left," she told him. "Otherwise—" She stopped, then murmured, "David?"

He had no tongue. His mind was in a struggle to regain itself.

"What is it?" Marianna sounded worried now. "Are you all right?"

David filled his lungs with fetid storeroom air. "Go—" he muttered.

"What?"

He swallowed hard. "Go back," he said. He couldn't recognize his voice.

She stood in fixed silence for a while; was it five seconds, ten? He couldn't tell. At last she backed off. David waited until there was a gap of several yards between the doorway and her, then stood on trembling legs and edged into the studio. Suddenly faint, he leaned against the wall.

"David, what is it?" she asked.

He shook his head infirmly. Why do you appear like that? he heard his mind demanding. Still, there was illumination now. This wasn't darkness, yet she stood before him, evidently physical. Conviction oscillated in his mind.

"What did she say to you?"

He started. "What?"

"What did she tell you about me?"

David set himself. "Why is that—?" Again, his voice failed and he drew in breath convulsively. "Why is that painting dated 1937?"

"So that's it." Marianna's smile was harsh, embittered. "She told you that I'm a ghost."

He stared at her in shock; again, his mind reversed itself.

"Didn't she?"

"Well—" He couldn't seem to form a thought. Like obstructed machinery, his brain felt jammed, grinding ineffectively.

Marianna turned away and moved to the couch. Settling on its shadow-hooded curtain, she began to stare across the room. David watched her in bewilderment.

"I'd hoped—" she started.

David waited. "What?" he finally asked.

She turned to look at him. "That I wouldn't have to tell you."

"Tell me—?"

Marianna sighed. "Come sit beside me."

He didn't move and, after several moments, Marianna turned away again. "You believed her, every word," she said.

"Marianna—" David drew in rallying breath. "Are you telling me—?"

"—that I'm not what she said?" She shook her head despondently. "David, do I have to *tell* you?"

"Marianna, I didn't believe her; not at all. You think I want to believe a thing like that? But that painting *is* dated 1937. Tell me why."

"Because that's the year it was painted."

His head began to swim again. "Of you?" he asked.

"I'm twenty-three years old, David."

"But . . . you told me—"

"I was teasing you."

"Why?"

"I didn't know you." Marianna shrugged. "I wasn't sure I wanted to know you."

David felt the muscles in his chest and arms begin to loosen. "And Terry Lawrence?" he asked.

"What about him?"

"You met him last summer?"

"Yes."

"How old is he?"

"Twenty-seven."

"Marianna—!" David glared at her in furious confusion. "How can he be twenty-seven? For God's sake, he could have a son that age!"

Her look was patient. "Yes; he could," she said.

"Oh, for—" David hissed, disgusted at himself. He felt like an idiot. A classic demonstration of cliche thinking, he thought. He'd been immersed in video dialectics far too long. Crossing the studio, he sat beside her. "And the woman in the painting?"

"My mother."

"Mrs. Brentwood." Revelation flooded through his mind. It hadn't been an actress she'd resembled at all. "You do live on the bluff then."

Marianna nodded.

"Why did you tell me you didn't? Never mind; I know. You weren't sure you wanted to know me."

She shook her head. "That wasn't the reason."

"What then?"

"I didn't want you to meet her." Marianna's shoulders bowed. "But now you have."

She sounded so defeated that, on impulse, David put his hand on hers. "It doesn't matter," he assured her.

"It doesn't?" Marianna looked up eagerly. "Nothing's changed?"

He started to reply, then checked himself; he'd consider that part later. "Tell me why your mother tried to make me think you're a—" He finished with a scoffing noise; the very word affronted him.

Marianna looked at him intently. He hoped she wasn't going to mention that he'd changed the subject. "Why did she?" he pressed.

"To frighten you away."

David noticed that his hand was still on hers and drew it back. "Why?" he asked.

"So I'd be alone again."

"I don't understand."

Marianna averted her face. "She hates me, David," she said. "She's hated me so long that—" She shook her head. "—I can't remember when it started."

"Why should she hate you?"

Marianna looked distressed. "What can I say that won't make me sound terrible?" she asked. She faced him. "She's my mother, David. I don't want to speak against her."

"She's spoken against you."

"I know, but—" Again she shook her head. "She isn't normal. The things she believes . . ."

"About the dead?"

Marianna shuddered. "Please."

"I'm sorry." David patted her back, then drew his hand away skittishly as the urge to stroke her rose in him. He felt his stomach muscles tensing and resisted it; he knew exactly what that meant now. "Why does she hate you?" he asked.

"Because I'm young," she said. "Because—" Her expression grew tormented. "—She says I have the beauty she lost."

David winced. The picture was depressingly complete now: A beautiful but selfish and vindictive woman resenting her own daughter for reminding her that she was growing old; jealousy begetting hatred and, at last, derangement. That was what he'd seen revealed in Mrs. Brentwood's eyes, heard trembling in her voice—a spiteful malevolence boiling in the depths of her.

"Did she frighten away Terry Lawrence's son?" he asked.

"Probably," she murmured.

David frowned. "Why do you live with her then?" he asked.

"I have to."

"Why?"

She stared at her hands. "I'm afraid, if I leave, she'll—"

"Kill herself?" he provided after several moments.

Marianna closed her eyes. "She's sick, David. She's so very sick."

Suddenly she pressed against him. "Hold me, please," she begged. He hesitated as she clung to him. "I need you. Please don't be afraid of me."

"Afraid?" His laugh was stricken. "Good God, you don't still think I'm afraid of you?" He put his arms around her. "Marianna." Poor, unhappy child, he thought. That's what she was; a child in a woman's body, earthbound in the far more grievous sense that she was bound to the carnal, seeking to derive all comfort and enjoyment from her flesh. Dear God, he thought unhappily; and he, with his own world of problems, had been fool enough to enter hers. She needed so much help and understanding, so much love, that even the lifetime of a younger man devoted solely to her welfare might not be sufficient. As for him—

He closed his eyes and felt the familiar assault of guilt. How irresponsible is the flesh, he thought; how negligent and greedy. He should never have begun with her. By doing so, he'd only made the tangled pattern of her life a little more disordered.

He tightened as she rubbed against him. "Love me, David," she whispered. "Make me forget."

"No." He spoke without thought.

Marianna sat up quickly, looking at him in dismay.

"I mean—" He broke off, feeling sick with fault. "It's not enough to just forget your problems, Marianna. You have to solve them." He felt contemptible for speaking this way; still, it was the truth. "You have to face reality, and—"

"No!" She cried out with such explosive vehemence that David felt himself recoil. "I won't! I won't!" She glared at him, the hatred in her face appalling him. Until that moment, he had never truly known the meaning of the phrase: "his blood ran cold."

"I want your body," she muttered, "I want to forget."

David stared at her dumbly, aware—for the first time it seemed—that she was virtually a sealed book to him. Her reaction had been so abrupt, so violent and unexpected that, at once, he was afraid of her again. She's mad, he thought. He felt, somehow, incredulous at his position. What in God's name was he doing here?

"Oh, David." Obviously, she'd noted his expression, for her tone was pained, repentant now. He shivered as she took his hands. "I'm sorry, darling. Please forgive me." She kissed the hands and held them to her cheeks. "It's only that I love you so, I lose my mind when you reject me."

"Marianna—"

"Please make love to me, David."

He couldn't speak.

"I'll make it nice for you. Here; feel how soft I am." She pressed his hands against her breasts. "You know I'm yours. Do anything you want with me." She pulled back. "Here, I'll take my sweater off so you can see them."

"Marianna, no!" He spoke through clenching teeth, his eyes closed tightly. Nausea billowed in his stomach. Even now, he wanted her; God in heaven, *even now*. Jarring to his feet, he hurried for the door, then stopped and turned. "I'm leaving, Marianna. I'm going home with my wife."

He drew in faltering breath. "I feel ashamed for having made your life more painful than it is already. For having used you to—absolve my own shortcomings. I apologize most humbly to you. But I have to leave. My responsibility is to my marriage. I wish I could help you, but I can't. You need much more than I could ever give."

They gazed at each other in silence. She *is* a ghost, he thought; the pitiful ghost of what she might have been. "Please don't hate me," he said. "I never meant to hurt you; that, I swear."

He felt himself begin to tighten as she stood and walked across the studio. She stopped before him. Unaccountably, she smiled; the smile that had bewitched him. "I don't hate you, David," she said cheerfully. Rising on her toes, she kissed his cheek. "Have a good trip."

He watched her as she moved away, a mixture of

emotions wresting him—sorrow and remorse and, in spite of everything, disappointment at her casual farewell. He heard her voice repeating, in his mind: It's only that I love you so, I lose my mind when you reject me. If she'd really meant it, how could she—?

He closed his eyes, grimacing. Vanity of vanities, he thought. Sighing, he waited for the sound of the closing door. When it came, he opened his eyes, listening to her footsteps on the stairs. Impulsively, he moved to the door and opened it. He heard her walk across the living room. The front door closed. He was not prepared for the burst of pain it caused him. He was going to miss her. She was ill. It was nothing but infatuation. His decision was the right one. Nonetheless, he'd miss her. What was that phrase from *Cyrano*? How well it applied to her. *That wind of terrible and jealous beauty blowing over me—that dark fire, that music . . .*

He whispered, "Marianna." Then, "Goodbye."

He was waiting in the living room when Ellen returned; as she opened the door, he rose from the sofa. Ellen stopped and looked at him in curious surprise. He swallowed. "Hi."

She didn't answer.

David hesitated, gestured toward the sofa. "Sit?"

Without a word, she crossed the room and settled on the sofa. He sat beside her.

Silence. David drew in strained breath. "Let's go home," he said.

Ellen watched him guardedly.

"It was a mistake to come here."

"Maybe not."

He started. "What?"

"Would we be better off if nothing had been said?"

He sighed, then, after several moments, shook his head. "No; it's better they were said. But . . . well, they *are* said now, the problem's in the open. Can't we settle it at home?"

She didn't speak.

"This place isn't right for it," he said. "It's true; you can't go home again."

"Is that what you think we were trying to do?"

"Yes." He nodded slowly. "I think we somehow had the feeling that what we'd lost might still be here in Logan Beach."

She looked at him a while before she lowered her gaze. "Perhaps you're right."

"Then let's go home."

"Home." She spoke the word as though it represented some impossible goal. David took her hand. "We can work it out," he said.

"But *will* we work it out?" Her look was one of pleading. "Or will we just . . . settle back in?"

He shook his head. "We couldn't if we wanted to."

"You sound almost disappointed."

"No." He smiled dejectedly. "Well, maybe a little. It was peaceful."

"And unreal."

"I guess." He looked at her inquiringly. "You don't regret the change at all then?"

"I regret that it came so late," she said, "I regret that we held it back."

David took his hand away, a wave of discouragement oppressing him. "You make it sound as if our marriage has been a fraud."

"I don't mean to." Ellen's tone was milder now though not placating. "It's only in the past few years that the pretending grew painful. Which brought on

Julia." She sat up straight. "As I said before: probably, I've put it all too harshly. All I wanted to convey was that we had a problem that couldn't be ignored any more."

"All right." He nodded once. "We won't ignore it anymore. We'll solve it; but at home, not here."

Ellen looked disturbed. "Can't we even start here?"

"I don't think so." David held himself in check. "It's—distracting, unfamiliar."

She didn't reply and he wondered, almost fearfully, what she was thinking. "Is that unfair?" he asked. "To want to settle it in our own home?"

"You don't even want to talk about it here?"

"Right now, you mean?"

"Yes."

"Well—sure; of course. I don't mean we have to board the plane in twenty minutes." He didn't dare press any harder for fear that his anxiety would seem undue. "I just mean, I think we ought to leave some time today; go home, really get to work on this."

Ellen sighed. "If you feel it's that important."

"Well—" If there was some alternative, he thought. He brightened as it came to him. "Look, we don't have to go back home immediately, if that's what bothers you. We can go some other place—"

She interrupted. "What would be the point of that?"

David felt himself tightening. "Well—" He shrugged. "So we wouldn't have to hurry home."

"But—" She gestured with exasperation. "Why not here then? This is where it all—opened up."

He drew in shuddering breath. "I just don't like it here."

"Why? Because it opened up here?"

"No." He looked distressed. "Well, maybe; I don't know."

Ellen sighed defeatedly. "Oh, David." She stared at her hands. "Is it really the location that bothers you?"

He didn't understand.

"Or is it the problem? Is that what you want to get away from?" She looked up. "Permanently, I mean."

David closed his eyes. There seemed to be a dreadful weight across his shoulders and he let them slump beneath it. "Do *you*?" he asked.

She didn't answer. Silence filled the room.

"I don't know," she said, finally. "I feel . . . extraneous, somehow. As if I've served my purpose and it doesn't really matter what I want anymore."

He looked at her in pained surprise; he'd never heard her sound so lost before. He wanted to take her hand again, console her; but something kept him from it.

"The more we talk," she said, "the more I get the feeling that our marriage, in the last few years, has been like an unsuccessful game of charades—each of us trying, in vain, to guess what the other was trying to convey." She turned to him. "Even so, I never felt as far away from you as I do right now."

He watched her stand and move across the room. She stopped at the foot of the stairs. "I'll go up and pack," she told him in a tired voice. "We'll go back to Sherman Oaks. We'll see about a divorce."

He shuddered. *"No."*

She looked at him in silence. He began to wonder, vaguely, if his eyes were going bad, she seemed to shimmer so before him. "No," he murmured. He shook his head, staring at her through a gelatinous film.

She seemed to drift across the room to touch his cheeks in wonder. "David?"

"No."

"You don't want it that way?"

"No."

"You want us to go on?"

He had only the strength to stretch out his hand for her.

"David." Suddenly, she was beside him, in his arms, her arms around him, her cheek pressed to his, her tears spilling across his face.

"Don't leave me, El," he begged.

"I won't, I won't."

"I need you. Please don't leave me."

"David. Oh, my sweetheart; David, David. I won't leave you. Not if you need me, never if you need me." She kissed his face and lips with joy.

David pressed his face into her hair and held her tightly. This is right, he thought; the rightness of it seemed to bathe his mind and body with a healing warmth. This is my love, my heart. How could he have doubted it? It was so clear. The passion he felt for her was so entirely different from that which he had felt for Julia, certainly for Marianna. This, too, was physical; yet, somehow, it transcended flesh, adding to it, the dimension of his mind; perhaps, his soul.

That's it! he thought. The realization struck him with awe. That was the solution, the combination, the Answer: to lend meaning to the body's appetite by giving it the motivation of unselfish love, expressing spirit through flesh. He'd thought of it before but now he knew it. He trembled at the concept—so violently that Ellen looked at him anxiously.

"What is it?"

"Nothing." David clung to her. His laugh was broken. "Nothing? My God, everything!" He shook his head, astonished. Was this inspiration? Was this the feeling of the self release which he had read about? His body seemed not gone, still with him but securely in its place now, not dominating any more, not the control but the instrument to be controlled; on it he could play whatever music he chose. He shut his eyes, feeling dizzy. Surely, this euphoria could not go on.

It didn't. Like a dazzling mantle thrown across him, then removed, the feeling lifted, gone beyond him. He could see again. He looked at Ellen. "Wow," he said.

"Wow?" She smiled.

"I just went cosmic."

"I don't—"

"—Understand? Neither do I but it was great." He held her close. "And it was all because of you. I don't know how but it was."

Whispering his name, she clung to him. "I love you so."

"Oh, I more than love you," David said. "I exist because of you." He kissed her lips. "Whatever that means; don't ask me, I don't know. The feeling's gone. I had it though and it was marvelous, it really was. I wish the same for you."

He stood and drew her up. Reality was back again, everything in proper place. "Come on," he said. "Let's get our stuff and head for home. There's a lot to do."

"All right, darling."

They moved for the stairs, arms around each other. "Look at us," she said. She brushed the tears from David's cheeks, her own. "A couple of boo-hoos."

"We were crying with love," he said. Remarkable, he thought. Until this moment, he would never have believed that he could speak such words and not feel self-conscious. Now, he only thought how true they were. "It's going to be all right," he said. "We're going to find the answer."

"I want to find it," Ellen said. "With you."

"Oh, definitely with me. That's in the books." He kissed her lightly on the cheek.

They started up the stairs. Amazingly, his step was buoyant; he didn't feel exhausted anymore. "Here, blow your nose," he said, holding up his handkerchief.

"I can't get over it," she said. "Here, I thought that everything was over; that you didn't love me, that you wanted to leave."

"I do love you," he said, "I'll *never* leave."

Her arm drew tight around him. "Don't."

"Never." He believed it too. It was incredible how positive he felt; how secure. Another cliché phrase, he thought; abused but apt: It was as though a weight had been lifted from his shoulders. That was how he felt—disburdened, confident. There wasn't even a twinge as they passed the studio. That was finished; a destructive yet enlightening episode. He did not regret it now except to the degree that it had injured Marianna.

He smiled. "One good thing; we'll be there when the baby comes."

She nodded, smiling. David looked at her more closely. "Talk about *me*," he said, concerned. "You look tired yourself."

"I am; a little bit." She leaned her head on his shoulder as they finished climbing the stairs. "Relief, I think. It's been a rough few days."

"I know." He squeezed her.

As they entered the bedroom, David noticed how

vague her expression was becoming. "You sure you're all right?" he asked.

"Sure." She patted his cheek. "It's just reaction. And that walk. I kept on going as if there was no tomorrow. I shouldn't have gotten up so early."

"Poor baby." David led her to the bed. "Here; sit. I'll do the packing."

She made no objection, sinking to the mattress with a groan. "Oh," she murmured. She smiled at him. "I feel a little weak, old boy."

"What did you eat this morning?"

"An oatmeal cookie."

"Ellen Audrey." Bending, he kissed the top of her head. "As soon as we're out of here, we're going to stop at a restaurant and get you a nice, big, heavily caloric meal."

"I'm not really hungry." Ellen sighed. "Just a little tired." She started to rise but David held her back. "I'll pack," he said.

"I don't want you to have to do it all."

"There's not that much to do. Here." Kneeling, he removed her shoes, then, standing again, lifted her legs and swung them toward the bed. She fell on the pillow with a tired grunt. "Feels good," she said. She reached out and took his hand. "I'll just rest a little. Then I'll pack."

"Don't worry about it."

"Don't you do it," Ellen said. "Here, lie beside me. We'll pack together in a little while."

David sat beside her and stroked her hair. "I want to get home with you," he told her. "We have a passel of years to catch up on."

"I love you, David."

He leaned over and kissed her gently. "And I love you," he said. "Some day I'll tell you just how much."

"Tell me now!"

"No, no. It would turn your head."

Ellen's smile was drowsy. "I could use a little head turning."

He ran a finger down the bridge of her nose. "Let's just say I couldn't cut the ice without you."

"Sure you could."

"No." He shook his head. "I couldn't. Really." He kissed her again. "Take a little rest now," he said. "I'll pack and then we'll go."

"All right." She stroked his cheek. "It'll be nice to get home." She yawned. "We'd better call Mark."

"We'll phone him from the airport." He grinned. "Give him a chance to get his women out of the house."

She smiled. "That's awful," she murmured.

"You rest now." He patted her cheek.

Ellen reached across her shoulder to touch one of the five X's on the headboard. "Wonder who made them," she murmured.

"Don't know, love." Standing, David crossed to the closet and opened the door. He pulled both suitcases off the shelf and turned back. "I imagine there's a flight about six or seven we can—"

He stopped and, putting the two suitcases on top of the bureau, moved back to the bed. Ellen was already asleep. He smiled at her. An angel, he thought. She really was. He shuddered at the thought that he'd almost left her. How could he have been so blind?

With care, he drew the comforter across her. She didn't stir. Poor kid, he thought. She must have been physically and mentally exhausted by all this. He'd make it up to her.

Smiling, he turned and walked to the bureau. Setting one of the suitcases on the floor, he opened the other on top of the bureau and began to pack in Ellen's belongings. Little Ellen Audrey, he thought. He patted her clothes as he put them in the suitcase. She was good for him. It was appalling to consider that he might have left her for Marianna. What a nightmare that would have been.

"Amen," he muttered.

The room was silent except for the rustling of clothes being packed; even the pounding of the surf seemed distant and muffled. David began to think about his flash of "exaltation" and what bizarre chemistry might have brought it about. Now that it was past, it was simpler to discredit. Not that it hadn't been electrifying; moments he would not have missed for anything. But that it had occurred within the realm of inspiration was more than improbable. He was David Cooper, TV hack, not some heaven-bent mystic.

What had, likely, hit him was a rush of gratified response at making up with Ellen. After all, they'd been in serious marital trouble for a long time. Add Julia to that. Add, to that, his liaison with Marianna in this very house, his consequent guilt and depression. Small wonder that, in making peace with Ellen so unexpectedly, he felt illumined by a burst of inner light, uplifted by the purging of that heavy guilt, the overbearing depression.

Not that he felt white-washed. Still, he definitely did feel as if a burden had been taken from him. So much so that perceptions of every kind seemed to be occurring to him where, before, there had been nothing but indifference.

Why was it, for instance, that, except on rare occasions in the past few years, he'd been unable to express, in physical terms, his love for Ellen? In their early years, there had existed, in their lovemaking, an atmosphere of romantic tenderness. True, it may have been delusive but both of them had believed in it.

Then it had faded. It had faded for other couples too, of course; reality was always cruel to dreamlike sentiment. In their case, though, the fading had resulted, not in usual boredom, but in a division of rapport. Their mental relationship had continued soundly; he liked Ellen, enjoyed her company, was proud to be her husband.

On the other hand, their physical relationship had begun to drift, separating from the basic substance of their marriage until it was virtually a relationship in itself. An unregenerative relationship, however, not viable enough to grow or ripen. A relationship in which—to keep it artificially alive—he had created constant, re-kindling stimulations. In time, that relationship had become, for him, rather than an overall fulfillment, a search for erotic variations.

He had sensed this many times but, fighting back, had managed to convince himself that this was sexual emancipation, adult and unconstrained. That the search had grown more intemperate by the year had only made him more defensive, more stubbornly determined that the search was justified.

No wonder, then, that Marianna had attracted him, being nothing less than the ultimate objective of this search: an exotic wanton who expected no emotional responsibility, who wanted and encouraged only self-indulgence. David shook his head. And he had been her instant and compliant partner.

Why?

Perhaps, because he hadn't lost the ability to express love in physical terms, but, rather, had never possessed it at all. Was that surprising really? His parents had separated when he was ten. An only child, he had been raised with intense protectiveness by his mother. She'd been devoted to him, yes, but, because his father had repelled her and because she was timid and withdrawn, she'd seen fit to make of sex, a shunned topic; shunned, he had sensed as a boy, because it was too vulgar and distasteful for her to examine—therefore, because he identified with her, too vulgar and distasteful for him to examine either. A secret; a taboo. She'd been affectionate and loving, but never with the slightest hint they were male and female. The schism was complete. On one side there was love, direct and clean. On the other side there was sex, devious and, by implication, dirty. He had grown to manhood never appreciating that the two should be one. Now, after all this time, he had to form connective tissue between them, for he knew that one without the other was inadequate and empty. Sex had to be more than the coupling of unrelated animals. It had to be the ultimate exchange of love between a man and a woman.

He blinked to find himself staring at his reflection in the bureau mirror. Now which way? he asked the somber visaged man before him.

"Forward, I hope," he murmured.

Hurriedly, he finished packing. The suitcases filled and shut, he set them by the door and returned to the bed. Ellen was sound asleep, her breathing deep and regular. He wanted to wake her and start for home but didn't have the heart. She looked so peaceful. He'd let her rest a while; she needed it.

He sat on the rocking chair and checked his watch. Almost four-thirty. He blew out fretful breath. Already, the light was fading. Maybe he should wake her after all. Allowing an hour to an hour and a half for the drive to the airport plus time for a restaurant stop didn't give them much leeway. As he recalled, there was a flight for Los Angeles around seven. It was unlikely they could make it unless he woke her now.

Oh, well. He shrugged. What were a few hours more or less? There was probably a late flight. The main thing was that they were going home. He relaxed and looked at Ellen's face. I love you very much, he thought. How marvelous that he should feel this way after all these years. It made his first infatuation for her seem childish and incognizant. This was based on knowledge, that on self-gratifying reverie.

He closed his eyes and listened to the muted booming of the surf. That I can do without for a long time, he thought. He considered, briefly, getting up to load the car, taking everything out of the house except Ellen and himself. He yawned. It could wait until she woke up. He smiled to himself. Mark would be surprised to see them; Linda too. Wonder if it's going to be a boy or a girl, he thought. Grandpa Dave, that lovable old coot. He made an amused sound. Him a grandfather. How ridiculous. He felt too young. He was going home with his child bride. Start out fresh. Years ahead of them. Joy. Contentment. Ellen. Home. Tonight.

Jerking up his head, he stared into the darkness. What the hell—?

He looked around, appalled, then raised his left arm which had gone to sleep, pinned between his body and the chair arm. Blinking hard, he focused on the hands of his watch. It was nine twenty-one. He groaned. "Oh, Christ." Standing with a crackle of bones, he felt his way to the nearest bedside table and turned on the lamp.

Ellen was still asleep, lying in the same position. David reached down to wake her, then withdrew his hand. He'd load the car first, straighten up the house; let her sleep until the last possible moment. Turning, he walked to the suitcases. There he hesitated, wondering if they ought to leave in the morning instead. Surely, there would be no flight available by the time they reached the airport.

No damn it, they were leaving now. If there wasn't a flight until morning, they'd rent a room near the airport. The way he felt, he was prepared to sit all night in the waiting room if he had to. Picking up the suitcases, he moved into the hall, set one of them down long enough to switch on the overhead light, then picked it up again and started downstairs.

Crossing the living room, he opened the front door and carried the luggage outside. The air was still and cold; well below freezing, he estimated. His breath steamed whitely as he unlocked the car trunk and loaded in the suitcases. The slam of the lid as he closed it sounded loud and sharp.

Shivering, he hurried back into the house and turned on one of the living room lamps. As he moved about the room in search of their belongings, he began to realize how hungry he was; not that it was strange, considering how little he'd eaten in the past few days. He picked up sweaters, jackets, some oatmeal cookies. Eating one of them, he carried everything to the door and dumped it on the floor. He'd make a pile and carry it all to the car later.

As quickly as he could, he moved around the room again, emptying ashtrays into the fireplace, straightening furniture and cushions, laying the bulk of the *Times* on the raised hearth; let some future tenant use it to ignite some future fire. It made him feel strange to realize that other men would probably stay here, encounter Marianna and become involved with her. He shook himself. So what? It wasn't his concern anymore. He looked around. The room was in order now. That left the kitchen, the bathroom and bedroom.

Moving into the kitchen, he switched on the light and picked up the carton they'd been using for rubbish. He carried it into the living room, emptied the trash inside the fireplace and lit it. Returning to the kitchen, he set the carton on the table and began to load it with remaining groceries. We really should leave them, he thought. Certainly, they couldn't take them on the plane. Still, there might not be another tenant for a long time; they couldn't very well leave it to rot. He cleaned out the refrigerator and cupboard, his stomach growling at the sight of food. If only there was time to fry himself some eggs, make some toast and coffee.

He closed his mind to the thought. Ellen was hungry too; he'd wait until they reached a restaurant. The atmosphere there would be more conducive to dining anyway. He pulled out the refrigerator plug, removed the ice trays and put them in the sink.

"Oh, nuts." There were dishes to be washed; he stared at them in aggravation. Sighing, then, he twisted the drain cup into place and began to run hot water, adding a capful of liquid soap. He stared at the foaming surface until it covered the dishes, then turning off the faucet, washed and rinsed the dishes, propping them in the rack.

Drying his hands, he turned to the table and took a chocolate cookie from its bag inside the carton. He looked around the kitchen. Good enough, he thought. He grunted in somber amusement as a thought occured to him. All those arguments his mother and father had avoided when he'd entered all those kitchens in the past; all the arguments his mother had not permitted him to have with her. He'd hated those evasions bitterly and, yet, he'd done the very same thing to Ellen—avoided arguments in order to maintain an atmosphere of peace, however fraudulant. He shook his head. Things rub off, he thought; even the things you despise.

He lifted the carton and moved to the doorway, turned to run a final gaze around the room. It was tidy, clean. Goodbye, kitchen, he thought. He remembered the first moment they'd entered it; it had been like an icebox. By tomorrow afternoon, the heat turned off, it would be the same. Flicking down the light switch with his left elbow, he backed through the doorway, carried the carton to the front door and set it down.

As he headed for the stairs, he noticed the two coffee mugs on the dining alcove table and, groaning, changed direction, picked them up and carried them into the kitchen, setting them in the sink. Wash 'em yourself, he thought.

Ellen didn't stir as he sat beside her on the bed. "Honey?" He put his hand on her shoulder and shook it gently. She failed to respond and he shook her harder. "Ellen?"

She moaned a little, turning her head on the pillow.

"Come on, honey." He shook her again. "Time to go home."

She mumbled something that he couldn't make out; then she was asleep again. David grimaced. "Ellen?" He patted her cheek. "Come on. It's time to go."

She rolled onto her side, her back to him. He waited a few seconds, then turned her onto her back again. "Wake *up*, my dear, my darling."

Ellen's eyelids fluttered, opening part-way. She peered at him groggily.

"It's time to go."

She grunted, stared. After several moments, her eyelids fell shut again.

"Ellen?"

She opened her eyes.

"Don't you want to go?"

"Time's't?"

He checked his watch. "Almost ten."

She grunted. "Late."

"I know it's late. That's why we have—to"

He broke off, astonished. Her eyes were closed again.

"Ellen?"

"Tired." She twisted onto her side again.

He stared at her in silence. For a moment, he had the uneasy feeling that they weren't going to leave until Thursday after all; that he was going to see Marianna again, that every gain would be lost. Frightened, he reached out to shake her violently, then drew his hand back. Actually, it made no sense to leave now. She was, obviously, exhausted. He should let her get a good night's sleep before they left.

He clucked. He'd let her sleep, wake her up at dawn.

That way they'd be in Los Angeles by late tomorrow morning; early afternoon at the most.

He watched her for a while, then decided that he may as well go down and fry himself some eggs. Standing, he turned out the lamp and moved into the hall. He took their toilet articles from the bathroom and trudged down the stairs. The edge was off their departure, that was certain. Leaving in the morning would be an anti-climax.

He put the toilet articles on the pile of clothes, carried the carton of food back into the kitchen, and turned on the light. He frowned at the thought of re-using the frying pan, a dish and mug, silverware, a spatula, the coffee pot. He'd make himself a sandwich.

Sitting at the table, he took two slices of wheat bread from their package and searched the carton for something to put between them. As he did, his hand closed over the neck of the martini-mix bottle. Good idea, he thought. He took it out, began standing to get a glass, then sat again. "Oh, no you don't." He'd drink from the bottle. By God, he'd even spread the margarine with his finger so he wouldn't have to wash a knife. He smiled as he unscrewed the top of the bottle and took a sip.

It hit his stomach with a jolt. "Yow!" He clenched his teeth and, hissing, set the bottle down. He looked in the carton again and found some cheese. Picking up the bottle he took another sip. That was better. Already, the warmth of the first sip was diffusing through his stomach and lower chest. "Stoke the furnace, man." He took another sip, a longer one.

Blinking, he put a slice of cheese between the two pieces of bread; he wouldn't even use margarine; save his finger. He took a bite of the sandwich. It tasted dry and made him cough; he took a drink of martini to wash it down. *Here comes the numbness, hurrah, hurrah!* His mind sang the words to the tune of a song he'd known in grade school: *Here Comes the Milkman.* He closed his eyes and felt the anaesthesia radiating through his body and head. By God, martinis were good, their language international. Gentlemen of the General Council, he addressed them, I hereby nominate the martini as United Nations Cocktail. Make it official and I guarantee you universal peace in twenty-four hours.

He took an extended drink from the bottle and set it down. Picking up the sandwich, he eyed it speculatively. "You do not appeal to me," he told it, putting it aside. He wasn't very hungry anyway. He tipped the bottle to his lips, then leaned back, sighing. After several moments, he raised his head again and took another drink. How much had there been in the bottle? There was about an inch left.

"Goombye, inch." He drained it off. "And to think, ladies and gentlemen of the radio audience," he announced, "I came down here for a fried egg. Now, I *am* a fried egg. I tell you, such a notion boggles the mind. We now return you to the *Adventures of Granpa Dave.*"

He hiccupped, frowned. Forgive me, other. His chin dropped to his chest. After a while, he lay both arms on the table and rested his head on them. "Take a snooze," he murmured. "Take a letter. My God, Miss Blodgett, I never saw you without your clothes on." He shifted in the chair, drawing in restless breath. Feel nervous, he thought. Want something; but what?

"Me?"

He sat up with a gasp.

"Behind you."

He twisted around. The swinging door was opened. In the dining alcove, just beyond the doorway, Marianna stood looking at him. David felt his stomach muscles wrench in.

She was naked.

He stared at her, unable to move. She drew in breath so that her heavy breasts hitched up, their nipples jutting darkly. "I came to say goodbye," she mocked.

He shook his head.

"Why not? No harm in it. Your wife's asleep; I checked. She's sound asleep. We have lots of time to say goodbye."

He felt himself shrinking from her. "I'm going home."

"Of course. I only came to say goodbye."

Helplessly, he ran his gaze down her body. "That's it, look at me," she said. He shuddered as she cupped a hand beneath each breast and held them up. "For you," she said. "Just one more time." Her teeth were clenched, her eyelids lowered halfway. "You know you want to. Only one more time. No harm in that." She drew back slowly.

No; I won't, he thought. But his mind was like a child before the burgeoning assurance of his flesh. He tried to shake it off but will would not direct his limbs. Standing dizzily, he weaved across the floor toward her.

"You want me, don't you?"

One more time, he thought. No harm in that. I'll be gone by morning. One more time, just one.

"Don't you, David?"

"Yes." Just one more time. He reach for her. She backed off and he stumbled after her into the living room, stepping across the jumble of her clothes. He had no mind now; he was body, flesh, an appetite.

"That's it; follow me. Follow like an animal. That's what we are. Animals. That's all that matters; being animals and enjoying it." She dropped to her knees, fell forward on her palms. *"Take me like an animal,"* she said.

Possessed, he staggered toward her, musk-thick fragrance like a mist around him, glutting his brain, the room revolving, darkening. Only her before him, white, luxuriant; an animal. He pulled at his clothes like unwanted scales. "Don't make me wait," she ordered. He fell to his knees behind her. "Now!" she screamed.

Then everything was lost in blinding, crazed desire as her lust devoured his body and, for all he knew or cared, his soul as well.

SUNDAY

It was not as waking usually was: floating upward through a depth of somnolence until one broke its surface and became aware. Today was different. For what seemed like hours, he remained submerged, hovering in a murky limbus between sleep and consciousness. He sensed the world above but could not rise to it. Each time he felt himself ascending, something dragged him down again. Neither dead nor living, he hung suspended in a soundless void.

Finally, there was sound: somewhere in the distance, waves crashing; close by, a wind-lashed spattering of rain on window glass. Slowly, David raised his weighted eyelids. Shadows wavered on the ceiling, shifting like gelatine. His head turned inchingly, then, uncontrolled, flopped over on its side. He stared at the window above the right-hand bookcase. It was covered by a streaming network of water. The fluctuating patterns held him in a daze of absorption.

He tried to push up, finding that he couldn't. Can't move; thought oozed, syrup-like, between the fissures of his brain. He considered looking at his watch but it was strapped around a bar of iron which had been his arm. He blinked and declined his gaze, staring dully at a row of books. His body slept on but he felt his mind awakening.

Earlier this morning (Was it morning now?) he'd woken to find himself, fetus-coiled and naked, on the rug. Wracked by chills, he'd struggled to his feet and managed to dress; his clothes had been scattered all around the room. He'd slumped onto a chair and rested for a while before excruciating thirst had driven him to labor up again and stumble to the kitchen where he'd gulped down five glasses of water, dripping it over his chin and the front of his clothes. After that, he'd hobbled back into the living room and collapsed across the sofa, losing consciousness immediately.

What time was it? He willed the raising of his arm, groaning at the effort it involved. The watch face blurred before his gaze, then shimmered into focus. Nine-sixteen. The arm fell heavily, his eyelids slipping shut. His brain began a backward somersault, turning over with protracted motion. He forced it upright, raised his lids again. He mustn't sleep.

Once, during basic training, he'd had a fist fight with another soldier from his barrack. The man had punched him repeatedly in the stomach and the next morning he'd felt as he did now, the muscles tender, sore and hot. He was thirsty again too; the tissues of his throat felt desiccated. He wondered if he had the strength to get a drink of water. Every muscle felt encased by lead. He was unable to distinguish where his body ended and the sofa began, all of it fused together into one ponderous mass. There was something else too; an aching in the back of his left leg. Only after concentration did he realize that it was the sciatic muscle hurting with that "toothache in the flesh" sensation he'd endured for sixteen months in 1967–68 when the disc had slipped out near the base of his spine.

David closed his eyes, grimacing. All the pain combined was not enough to dissipate the shame he felt. Once more, he'd broken faith with Ellen, his mind lost another battle. Lost? he thought, bitterly. There'd been no contest. Only when the dictates of his flesh had been obeyed had his mind appeared like some cowardly servant who had hidden when its master was in peril, cringing back, contrite and meek, when danger had passed.

He tried to stand; they had to get out of here. He couldn't even sit up. His limbs felt paralyzed, like the exanimate members of a paraplegic. He strained with all his might, hardly stirring. Finally, he slumped back, breathless. How could anyone be so exhausted?

You're exhausted, aren't you? You sleep too much. You have a dreadful thirst which cannot be relieved. Your solar plexus feels abused and tender. Did Mrs. Brentwood really know? Despite more than forty years of hard-headed logic, was it conceivable that Marianna *was* a ghost?

"Allright." He said it doggedly, teeth clenched. He had to consider it because it was conceivable. No matter what he thought or believed, there was evidence to support it.

The day they'd arrived, Ellen had chosen not to enter the studio. She'd stood outside and not been incapacitated by the cold. Yet, once inside the house, she'd suffered such a chill that he'd had to cover her and light a fire.

Evidence.

When Marianna first seduced him, he'd experienced an overwhelming sense of *wrongness.* True, it might have been no more than guilty conscience. At the same time, it might have been something else, deep inside of him, reacting to a trespass which eclipsed human morality.

That involuntary traction in his solar plexus whenever Marianna was around, more powerful the closer she came. That was not imagined; he knew it had occurred. What was it though? Only tension?—or something else entirely? That feeling he'd had when he'd gone to Ellen after his first debauchery with Marianna. Guilt alone? Or, conjoint with guilt, the need of a frightened child for solace?

Evidence.

Why had he felt so relieved when they'd left the house on Friday night? That wasn't rationalization; he had felt immeasurably better. Had it only been because he was delivered from the risk that Ellen might encounter Marianna? Or had the separation caused a fear which penetrated far more deeply? He recalled thinking, in the drug store and the car, that, if they returned to the house, something terrible was going to happen. Simple apprehension? Or a premonition of malignant danger?

His dread concerning his ability to satisfy Ellen. He'd never felt it before. Had it been some kind of culminating anxiety? Or had it been, instead, that he sensed himself being drained of vital energy? Why had he made love to her in the car? It hadn't been only for the purpose of erotic stimulation. He distinctly remembered thinking that it had to be there, that he couldn't gratify her at the house. He recalled the hideous sequence of moments later during which he'd been convinced that he was going mad. There'd been no logical reason for it; none at all.

Evidence.

That sense of ecstasy; that feeling of incredible release. He had convinced himself that it was nothing but relief at having settled his problem with Ellen. What if, it had been Marianna letting go? Hadn't Ellen grown exhausted immediately afterward and gone to sleep, preventing their departure from the house?

The evidence collapsed with that. There was no sense to the notion that Marianna could affect Ellen as well. Ellen didn't even know about her, had nothing to do with her. David closed his eyes, defeated. Why fight it? It was him; his lack, his failure. He couldn't pawn it off on the occult. It would be easier to believe that Marianna had no existence at all, that he'd suffered a hallucination.

He grasped at that straw too before discerning, with a somber smile, that it was hardly possible for Mrs. Brentwood to be subject to the same hallucination. Not that he wasn't a likely subject for a sexual fantasy—middle-aged, depressed, suffering from serious marital problems. Still, it wasn't that. It was him— perfectly sane but, in other respects, quite imperfect. He, too, was earthbound, pinioned to the flesh, only too willing an accomplice to its constant and inexorable demands.

Footsteps on the stairs. From somewhere, David found the strength to sit up. Was it Marianna? There was little reason to suppose that it was yet he feared that it might be, that she might have been upstairs with Ellen, told her everything. His fingers gouged in slowly at the sofa cushion as the footsteps neared.

Ellen stopped and looked at him, surprised. "Well, hi."

"Hi." He tried to sound untroubled; to reciprocate her smile as she crossed the room.

"How are you?" she asked.

"Fine."

She sat beside him and, as though it were a casual gesture rather than the agonizing movement of two, incredibly heavy burdens, he put his arms around her. Ellen kissed his cheek. "Good morning."

"Morning, El."

"It's sure a doozy of a day to leave, isn't it?"

He grunted. "Sure is."

"Did you sleep?"

"Not much."

"Oh; I'm sorry." She squeezed his hand. "Where did you sleep? Down here?"

"Mm-hmm." He hoped she wasn't going to ask him why. "Cat naps mostly."

Ellen kissed him on the cheek again. "You can make up for it tonight."

He couldn't visualize that far ahead.

"I'm sorry I conked out on you yesterday," she said. "I must have been more tired than I thought."

"That's all right. You needed it."

She studied his face. "How long have you been up?"

"An hour; two."

"That long." She looked surprised again. "You've eaten then."

He hesitated. "No."

"You haven't?"

"I had some coffee."

"You want some breakfast before we leave?"

Leave, he thought. The prospect seemed not only formidable but, somehow, unattainable.

"We could stop on the way to the airport if you'd rather," Ellen prompted.

"Oh, we may as well eat here," he answered. "Use up that food."

"Oh." She hesitated, nodded. "Okay; I'll cook it up." She looked around. "Where's your cup?"

He stared at her.

"Didn't you say you'd had coffee?"

"Oh; yeah. I washed the cup when I was done."

She nodded again and stood. As she headed for the kitchen, a pang of fear made David shiver. What was wrong with him? He didn't want to eat here; he wanted to leave. "Uh—"

Ellen turned. "Yes?"

"Would you bring me some water?" he asked.

She stood motionless.

"What is it?" he asked.

"Is something wrong?"

"No." He almost winced, his tone seemed so grotesquely cheerful. "Why do you ask?"

"I thought there might be."

"No."

She gazed at him a few more moments, then moved for the kitchen. Almost instantly, she turned back. "Maybe you should phone for reservations while I'm making breakfast."

"There's no hurry."

Ellen gazed at him again. Making him wonder if he looked as tired as he had the past few days. Anxiously, he scanned his mind for something to say that would make her realize he was all right. He was still trying when she turned away and went into the kitchen.

As the door swung shut, he slumped against the

sofa, all strength gone again. He closed his eyes and let his head loll clumsily. If only he could sleep. Twitching at the thought, he raised his head and stared determinedly into the fireplace. That he mustn't do.

He frowned, confused. He couldn't understand why he'd suggested eating breakfast here. Not only would it waste the time it took to prepare but there'd be dishes and utensils to clean again—and, already, it was almost ten o'clock. We have to go, he thought. He tried to stand to tell her but he couldn't.

When Ellen came back, carrying a glass of water he thought: Perhaps we'd better stay here today and get the utilities turned off. He almost suggested it before he caught himself. Nervously, he took the glass from her. "Thank you." He felt her eyes on him as he drank.

"You're sure you wouldn't rather eat on the way?" she asked.

"We have to use up that food," he heard himself reply, startled by the childish logic of his answer. "I mean—there's time. We've already missed the morning flight anyway."

"Is there an afternoon flight?"

"I imagine."

"We don't have a schedule with us?"

"I don't think so."

"Oh." She nodded, obviously disturbed. "And you don't think it's necessary to phone for a reservation?"

"There's time."

He had the uncomfortable impression that he'd sounded like an old man. As she stared at him, he broke the silence with the first idea that came to mind. "I'm sorry I finished that martini mix last night."

Ellen didn't answer at first; then she said. "I didn't know you had."

"You didn't see the empty bottle?"

"No."

"Come on." She was lying to him; that was obvious. He knew she didn't approve of his drinking.

"What do you mean?" she asked.

"You don't have to tactfully pretend you didn't see it."

Ellen looked perplexed. "David, I didn't see it. What are you trying to say?"

He stared at her blankly. After a while, he swallowed. "Nothing."

Ellen sat beside him. "I'm sure there's something wrong," she said.

"Why?"

"Because—" She frowned as if the answer were so obvious it needed no recital. "Are you telling me there isn't?"

"That's right." He drew in shaking breath. "There isn't."

He tried to think of something more to say but couldn't, his mind like a revolving kaleidoscope, fragments of thought tumbling into endless, fleeting combinations. She kept staring at him so intently that he clutched at one of them. "How come you don't wear nightgowns?" he asked.

"What?"

"You didn't hear?"

"I heard."

"Well?"

"I don't see what it has to do with—"

"It has everything to do with everything." He turned his face away, then looked at her irately. "You don't care to answer, is that it?"

"You really feel it's vital that you know right now?"

"I do."

"All right," she said. "I don't wear them because you don't want me to."

"What are you talking about?"

"I wore them for a long time, David; a *long* time. I tried to look as nice as I could for you." She shrugged. "But between—" She broke off.

"What?"

"Nothing."

"Between what?"

"David, this is not the time or place. We have to go home."

His teeth were set on edge now. "Between what?"

Ellen closed her eyes and drew in strengthening breath. "Between one night not caring how I looked and the next night wanting me to look like a whore, there simply wasn't any point in wearing nightgowns."

"Wanting you to—?" David looked astounded.

"You deny it?" Her eyes were open now, fixed challengingly on his. "Black Merry Widows? Black demi-bras? Black garter belts? Black silk stockings? Black high heeled shoes? What do you *think* they made me look like?"

"Perhaps an exciting woman," he replied. "Perhaps not." He looked at her coldly. "You slept in those things every other night, did you?"

"I wore them whenever you asked."

"And sometimes when I didn't."

"Because I knew you wanted it that way."

"But you were repelled by them."

"Not repelled, for God's sake! Are you making me out a prude now?"

"You said you were repelled by them."

"*You* said it!" Ellen shuddered with repressed fury.

"All I'm saying is that—once in a while, I would have liked to lie beside you in a frilly nightgown. Just lie there with your arms around me; quietly, peacefully. Your wife. Your *girl*." Her voice broke and she rose abruptly. "I'll make your breakfast."

"To hell with my breakfast!"

"You don't want any now?" Her reply was quiet, stripped of emotion.

"I don't want any now."

She nodded once. "Then there isn't any reason why we shouldn't leave, is there?"

David felt his stomach muscles jerking in.

"You do want to leave, don't you?" she asked.

He had no answer.

"You do want to leave, don't you?"

His smile was venomous. "I'll tell you when I know," he said.

Silence so encompassed him that it seemed as if he heard each separate raindrop drumming on the windows and was able to identify the cannonading roar of each wave breaking on the shore. He returned her gaze willfully, staring at her eyes until her face went out of focus.

He started as she looked around, spoke.

"What?"

Her voice was calm. "I asked where my jacket is."

"It's in the car."

"And the keys?"

He swallowed. "In the car."

She nodded once, politely. "Thank you." As she started toward the door, he felt a wrenching spasm in his heart. Don't leave! he thought.

She turned to look at him.

"I'm going to the nearest telephone," she told him

quietly. "I'm going to call home and see how Mark and Linda are. Then I'm going to call the airport and make reservations. After that, I'm going to come back and see if you're ready to leave." She paused. "If you're not," she said, "I'm going home without you." The door thumped shut and she was gone.

David felt as though he were about to rush to the door and fling it open, call to her: I didn't mean it! Let's go home right now! Then he heard the car being driven away and knew that it was too late.

He was alone in the house.

"No." He looked around, aghast. Was Marianna here?—about to have her way with him again? For a long while he sat in terrified anticipation. Only as minutes passed and nothing happened did he close his eyes, shoulders slumping with relief.

Which faded in moments. How could there be relief, his situation being what it was? He tried to understand what was happening but it made no sense to him. He wanted to leave, yet he'd instructed Ellen to make breakfast here. He wanted to go home, yet he'd acted as if he had no intention of doing so. He'd wanted to say specific things, yet been incapable of it. What it narrowed down to was that he was behaving in a manner inconsistent with his desires—to the point of uttering words which directly contradicted his will. In brief, he was displaying every symptom of a person under control. But whose control? Marianna's? He wouldn't accept that; it was just too much at variance with his convictions. Which left only one possibility: that the conflict came from his sub-conscious.

That his mind was slipping.

"No." He forced himself to stand and move for the kitchen, trying to ignore the bite of pain in his leg, the stiff, shuffling gait he was compelled to use. There was nothing wrong with his mind. It was guilt that made him act as he did.

He stopped abruptly, twisting around as a car drove up outside. She'd come back! An anxious smile pulled at his lips as he moved for the door. I'm sorry, Ellen. Let's go home right now. His fingers closed around the knob and pulled.

He stood unmoving as Mrs. Brentwood ran to the doorway and stopped. "Expecting me?" she asked, half smiling.

"I—" David shook his head, unable to finish.

She stepped into the house, her raincoat brushing against him, making him twitch. She turned to him. "Aren't you going to close the door?"

Swallowing, he pushed it shut.

"I passed your wife."

He waited.

"She's coming back, isn't she?"

"Yes."

"And both of you are leaving?"

David couldn't answer.

"Both of you are leaving, Mister Cooper?"

"Yes."

She looked relieved. "When I saw your car still parked outside this morning . . ."

He wondered why he felt such animosity toward her.

"Mister Cooper?"

"What?"

"You *are* leaving?"

He felt the skin drawn tight across his cheekbones. "Would you like it in writing?" he asked.

She winced. "Dear God, the truculence. Already, the truculence."

His fingers seemed to curl in of their own accord until the nails were digging at his palms. "I suppose that means something," he said.

"It means, my dear man, that, if you fail to leave this house today, you may never leave it. Sane, that is."

After a few moments, he snickered and turned away.

"Listen!" She grabbed his arm. "You are possessed! No matter how inane the notion seems to you, you *are* possessed; your will is almost gone." She dug her fingertips into his flesh until they hurt. "You had better listen to me, Mister Cooper. There is no antagonist on earth more ghastly than the dead who will not rest. Marianna is a twisted, blighted soul. All her life she thought of nothing but carnality. Terry Lawrence had no meaning to her other than providing her with one more body she could use—as she is using yours. Yes, I know that too," she added as he stiffened.

"Before she died, Marianna had an endless succession of lovers, each more vile than the one preceding—until, near the end, she wallowed in lust with men who were more animal than human—brutes, degenerates. The last of them—an alcoholic laborer who'd been in jail a dozen times for sex offenses—beat her up so savagely that, half-insane, she killed herself; drove both hands through one of the studio windows, cut her veins and bled to death. This is the creature who controls you, fascinates you. Oh, don't deny it. Spare me that, at least. Just leave this cottage."

David felt himself about to topple, the floor rising under him. "All that just because she's young?" he said, defensively. "Just because she has the beauty you lost?" He shook his head. "How you must hate her. Your own child."

"Oh." She spoke the word as though it were a groan of pain. "Dear God, dear God—*again*?" Her smile was bitter. "Well, why does it startle me?" she said. "It's not the first time. And, of course, you believed her; naturally, you would. She's such a skillful liar. How could you not believe her?"

"Which is to tell me, I presume, that you're not her mother."

Her laugh was harsh, astringent.

"My dear man," she said. "Marianna was my sister."

Again, that feeling of the floor beginning to elevate, tilt. He fought it off.

"I hadn't planned to tell you that," she said. "Actually, you're only the second tenant of this house I *have* told." She paused. "The other was that poor wretch who went insane. It did no good to tell him, of course. He didn't believe a word I said."

"Nor do I, Mrs. Brentwood."

She seemed to give up then, her expression becoming that of an opponent who had renounced all interest in the battle. David pressed in, strengthening his advantage. "I find it somewhat suspect that, again, you've given me no real evidence," he said. "Surely, it exists—especially if you're her sister. A certificate of death, for instance. Newspaper items."

"They exist," she said. "I have them in my house."

"Where they will, doubtless, remain," he broke, "unseen by anyone except yourself."

She shrugged.

"Forgive me if I speak my mind," he said. "But you must consider me an idiot. A ghost with flesh? With breath? *A ghost I could make love to?*"

Her lack of reaction flustered him. "How painfully ignorant you are," she said. "But, then, how could someone of your sort be expected to know that psychic literature abounds with authenticated cases of ghosts whose appearances—to all five senses of their viewers—were those of living people?" Her smile ridiculed him. "Including breath and lovemaking," she said.

He shuddered. "And, of course, they all wore clothes," he mocked, uneasily. "Walked on stairs and opened doors."

"And lifted objects and made shadows and strangled people," she appended. "Quite."

She raised her hands as if to mollify him. "Not seeking, for a moment, to dissuade you," she continued, "but it must be obvious—even to you—that, if Marianna not only doesn't care for you to know that she's a ghost but doesn't even choose to believe it herself, she would, accordingly, remove and put on clothes in your sight although she could, as easily, make them vanish and appear in seconds. She would open doors when she could, if she chose, pass through them like a vapor. She would walk on stairs even though she is capable of moving from place to place in an instant."

David's mind reeled back, impotently. He clutched for more defenses finding only one. Happily, it was irrefutable. He flung it into her face. "And could she, also, remove a locket and chain from around her neck and leave it overnight in my possession?"

Dear God, that smile again.

"An apport, Mister Cooper—a materialized object which can exist for indefinite periods of time. In this case, an object removed from my house—where it is at this moment, locked inside a jewel box in Marianna's room." She gestured casually. "But, of course, that's a lie. I made it up just now." She looked at him another moment before taking hold of the doorknob.

"One concluding lie," she said. "It just occurred to me; it's so unique I really must pass it along. Do you know why you feel exhausted?—Why your solar plexus aches?—Why you're so dehydrated? This will amuse you. Because you've been acting as a medium. The body you've been—making love to, as you so quaintly put it, has consisted, in every detail, of the cells in your own body. Isn't that a marvelous lie? Wait, I'll make it better. *You were aware of it all the time.* The sensation was that of drawing in your solar plexus. And, now, goodbye. Have fun."

She left the door ajar so that the cold wind rushed in, spraying the floor with rain. David stumbled across the room and closed it slowly. Turning back, he moved to the nearest chair and sank down on it. It isn't true, he told himself. It had been nothing but reverse psychology, the liar calling the lie a lie in order to imply its truth. They *were* lies though; all of them. They had to be because—

He gave it up. He simply didn't know anymore. All his mind would retain was the sickening notion that he may have been in essence, making love to his own flesh. If it were true, it meant that he had consummated, in literal terms, what, emotionally, he'd been doing all these years—holding personal gratification above all else.

"God . . ." He shut his eyes, aware of hot tears trickling down his cheeks yet hardly feeling them. I've got to leave this place. He clenched his teeth. If he could just hold on until Ellen got back. He could leave it all behind then, start off, fresh. Hang on, he pleaded with himself. She's coming back, she'll be here soon. Just hang on.

He jerked up his head as the front door closed. (Had he fallen asleep?) He stared at Ellen as she crossed the chair and stopped in front of him. His mind seemed vacant.

"The baby was born last night," she said. He started to speak but she cut him off. "The delivery was complicated and Linda's still in the hospital in serious condition."

David looked at her in silence. Yes, of course, he thought; we'll go immediately. "How serious?" he asked.

Ellen frowned. "Does it matter?" she asked. "Will it alter your decision about going?"

"I asked you a question."

"She may die, David." Hearing the break in her voice, he noticed suddenly—how could he have missed it?—that she was fighting back tears. My god, El, I'm sorry, he thought; of course we'll go. He sat mutely, staring at her. Speak, he thought, not knowing if it was in reference to her or to himself.

"David, are you going?" she demanded.

"No," he said. A burst of panic scourged his mind. I mean yes! he thought. Of course, I'll go!

Ellen looked appalled. "Even though she's in the hospital?" she asked. She gazed at him as if he'd been exposed to her as an imposter. "Even though she may die?"

"Get out of here," he heard himself answering. That

isn't me, he thought, terrified. I don't mean it, El. I want to go but—

"I don't understand you, David." She began to cry. "I just don't understand you anymore."

He wanted desperately to jump up, put his arms around her, comfort her; drive her to the airport and take her home. In the very act of wanting it, he heard his voice say, coldly, "Too bad." Ellen, help me! he thought.

"My God," she murmured. "What's happened to you?"

"Allow me to inform you," he said, his voice low-pitched, cunning. That isn't me! screamed his mind. "I finally know what I want. Not you. Not marriage—parenthood—*boredom.*" He felt his lips drawn back in a grin. No, he thought; God help me, no.

"Sex," he muttered. "Lust. You know what I mean? *Depravity.*" He felt the muscles tensing in his arms, felt them pushing him up from the chair. Ellen started backing off, a look of sick dismay on her face. "Get the picture? I'm sick and tired of your sanctimonious bitching." (No!) "I want women. *Women*: any kind I can get, old or young, I don't care. I want to glut myself on them; grovel in the mud with them." *(No!)* "Sluts! Whores! Pigs!" The words spouted from his lips like acid; he felt his body convulsed as he tracked her across the room. "I want obscenity! Orgies and defilement! Filth! Pollution!" His voice scaled upward to a shrill, demented screaming. *"God damn you, get the hell away from me before I kill you!"*

As he lunged for her, she stumbled and fell backward on the stairs, hitting her head. David's claw-like hands collided, fingers bending back and, tripping over Ellen's legs, he crashed to his left knee, crying out at the fiery explosion in his kneecap. Blinded by the pain, he flung his head back, gagging. Darkness swirled around him and he plunged to his right side, clutching at the knee with palsied fingers. *Up!* a voice commanded. He raised his head. Ellen was sprawled across the bottom steps, gaping at him, her expression one of horror. Oh, my God, he thought. He reached out with a shaking hand. "Ellen." He could barely speak, his voice turbid and strained—but, at last, his own. "Get me out of here. Something awful in this cottage. Not me." He sucked in wheezing breath. "Please take me home," he whispered hoarsely.

She was nodding. Wasn't she? He blinked and squinted at her. Yes! Nodding slowly, she was pushing to her feet. "All right," she said. "All right." She started backing up the stairs, weaving unsteadily. "All right."

David slumped to his side again, the coldness of the floorboards pressing at his cheek. It's going to be all right, he thought. She understands; she knows it wasn't me that said those things. Later, I'll explain it; later. He closed his eyes, reassurance flowing into him. He felt the muscles in his arms and legs unknotting. Relax, he thought. It's over now. He lay immobile, listening to the rain. Quiescence washed across him like a sun-warmed current. Wonderful, he thought; almost a repetition of the buoyant way he'd felt when—

David pushed up, grasping. Suddenly, the relaxation of his body terrified him. Dear God, he couldn't even feel the pain in his leg anymore! Lurching to his feet, he floundered up the stairs as rapidly as possible. It wasn't true; it couldn't be. "Ellen?" He called to her in dread. "Ellen!"

Just inside the bedroom doorway, he stumbled into

her jacket and froze, gaping at her. She was leaned against the headboard of the bed, half prone, half sitting. She'd pulled her skirt up past her hips, unbuttoned her blouse and, breathing hard, eyes widened, bright with craving, was tugging up her brassiere. Her breasts fell loose and clutching at them eagerly, she began to writhe on the mattress. As David watched in shock, she pulled both breasts toward her mouth, declined her chin and started licking at the hardened nipples, running her tongue around and over them, eyes half shut, short, animal-like gruntings in her throat. He moved across the room, staring at her unbelievingly. When he reached the bed, Ellen glanced up, then, with a lascivious smile, returned to her breasts, kissing and licking them with shameless absorption. His presence only seemed to stimulate her further.

"Ellen . . ." David felt as much embarrassed as dismayed. He'd never, in his life, seen a woman making love to herself, least of all his own wife. The sight unnerved and frightened him even though he was unable to suppress a tremor of distorted excitation. "Ellen, *don't*," he muttered.

She looked up. "Why? You want to do it yourself?" Before he could respond in any way, she dipped her head and started in again.

"Ellen!" He grabbed her hands and held them tightly. Jerking up her head, she glared at him. "Let go of me," she said, her voice malignant, coarse.

"Ellen, you don't know what you're doing."

Her laughter chilled him. "Idiot," she said. "You're the one who doesn't know." Unexpectedly, she jerked her hands free and seized her breasts again. Holding them upright, she stared at herself with a look of covetous longing. "To have a body," she said, "to be able to feel it and caress it. *A real body.*"

Horror pierced him to the heart. Struck dumb, he watched her as she twisted on the bed, abandoned to her craze of self adoring. He sensed his lips moving without sound, felt the word rising in his throat. At last it came. "Marianna?" He leaned over, trying to distinguish something in her face. "It's you, isn't it?"

She let her head thump back against the headboard, smiled at him. He felt nausea cloud his stomach. "Isn't it?"

She only smiled and asked "Who?"

He shuddered. "Don't."

"Who's Marianna?"

"Damn you!" David almost sobbed the words.

Unmoved, she looked at her body again, sliding back her feet until her knees were high, raising her hips. "My body," she said.

"Marianna!"

She dropped her trunk and, leaning back her head again, looked up, amused. "I don't know who this Marianna is," she chided, "but you must not like her very much."

He begged. "Don't do this, please don't do this."

"Do what?"

He closed his eyes, shivering convulsively. "Marianna, leave her be."

"You know?" she said. "I bet I can tell you what these five X's mean. I bet they mean that a certain someone got laid five times in one hour. I bet that's what it means; you want to bet?"

"Marianna, for God's sake!"

"Why do you keep calling me that?" she said. "I'm

your wife." She smiled at him wantonly. "You said you wanted sex; depravity. I'm going to give it to you—all you want. Orgies and defilement, that's what you said. Fine. I want it too. Why not? Why should I be moral anymore?" Her teeth clenched savagely and, rearing up her hips, she jerked off her underpants, kicking them aside. "That's what you want? Take it then! Glut yourself! You're married to a whore now, a pig!" Her face contorted, flushed, she grabbed for him with hands like blood-drained talons. "Grovel in the mud with your pig!" she snarled.

David backed off, paling, his expression one of dazed confusion. Ellen flung her legs across the mattress edge and, lurching upward, threw herself against him. "Now!" she raged. "I want it now!" He grabbed her wrists and started wrestling with her, struck with terror by the demoniac contortion of her face, the torrents of foul-mouthed language which spewed from her. "Stop it, Ellen!" But it wasn't Ellen, it was Marianna, it had to be. Still, he wasn't sure and, struggling with her, panic rising, he waited for her to break, burst into conscience-stricken tears, unmask herself. With increasing desperation, he searched her face for some revealing sign.

It failed to come. Unable to control him physically, she began to curse him, flogging his mind with a succession of the most virulent profanities he'd ever heard in his life. The brutality of them enervated his grip so that she was able to jerk one hand free and claw at his face with it; he gasped as her nails raked savagely across his cheek. The pain drove reactive strength into his arms and, grabbing her again, he squeezed her wrists as hard as he could, trying to make her cry, relent. If it was Ellen—but it wasn't—but if it was—yet it couldn't be—his mind rocked back and forth disord-eredly, unable to resolve itself.

Instead of crying, she ceased her struggles and leaned against him, making him think that she'd given up. Then, she started writhing. "Tear my clothes off," she muttered. "Hurt me." She licked his neck. "Rape me," she said.

With a faint, near delirious sob, David shoved her away, making her slip and fall. Instantly, she rolled onto her back and spread her legs apart, clasping her hands behind her neck. "All right, lover, give it to me." Baring teeth, she thrust her loins up, jerked them down, thrust them up again. "Let's go, you bastard, go!"

David whirled and ran, careening, toward the hall. As he staggered past the door, he saw a key protruding underneath the knob and, lurching around, pulled the door shut, cutting off the sight of her standing up, a look of fury on her face. His fingers trembled on the key; he barely managed to twist it before the knob was wrenched at from the other side. "Let me out, you son of a bitch!" she screamed. "If you won't give me what I want, let me find somebody else who will!" She pounded on the door with her fists. "God damn you, open up this door, you dirty fucking bastard!"

David's legs gave way; shuddering, he crumpled to his knees and leaned against the wall. Dear God, dear God, what had he done? If it was Marianna, he had paved the way for her to strike at Ellen and possess her. Worse, if it was really Ellen, his neglect and cruelty had driven her insane. He shook his head impotently. No, it couldn't be that; the mind did not give way that easily. He drove his fist against the floor, grimacing at the pain. It couldn't be that!

Inside the bedroom, Ellen beat at the door, shouting dementedly. David clenched his teeth and straightened up. It wasn't Ellen. He had to set his mind on that. In order to retain his sanity, he had to believe that it was Marianna in the bedroom, housed within the body of his wife. Which meant that only one person could help him now.

Pushing to his feet, he ran downstairs, pulled on his jacket and hurried out to the car. The key was still in the ignition slot. Starting the motor, he gunned the car away from the house and started up the hill toward the main road.

The mind betrays, he thought. Time and again, instinct had warned him that there was something wrong about Marianna. Yet, every time it had, he'd retreated automatically to what he had chosen to think of as logic, letting so-called rationality drive him further from the truth with every passing day. He winced, his fingers tensing on the wheel. And, with every passing day, Marianna had strengthened her hold on him.

Or had she?

David strained to freeze the pendulum and prevent it from swinging back again to "logic." It was Marianna he was fighting. "It *is*," he muttered.

He had just turned onto the hilltop road when the Bentley appeared around the curve ahead. "Thank God," he said. Honking the horn, he steered to the side of the road and stopped. As he pulled out the handbrake and switched off the motor, Mrs. Brentwood pulled the Bentley to the other side of the road and stopped. Pushing from the car, David slammed its door and dashed across the rain-swept road. Mrs. Brentwood lowered the window as he ran up.

"Are you going to the house?" he asked.

"I was bringing you those things you asked to see."

"It doesn't matter now," he said.

"Why? What's happened?"

David braced himself. "She's taken over my wife."

Mrs. Brentwood stared at him. "Oh, no," she murmured.

"I'll turn around and follow you," he told her. Wheeling, he ran across the road and got back into the car. Starting the engine, he glanced across his shoulder, then drove up the road a way and made a U-turn. As he started back, he frowned, a sense of indefinable alarm oppressing him. Mrs. Brentwood's car was in the same place, its motor still turned off.

Pulling up behind it, he waited anxiously; then, seeing that she wasn't going to move, he pushed outside and ran to her window. This time she didn't open it. She was sitting motionless, looking at her hands which were clasped together on her lap.

"Mrs. Brentwood?"

She neither answered nor turned. David stared at her, his insides going cold and tight. He tried to open the door but found it locked. Grimacing, he ran around the front of the car and pulled open the other door. "What's the matter?" he asked.

She looked at him without replying.

"What is it, Mrs. Brentwood?"

Her lips moved but no sound emerged. Quickly, David got inside and pulled the door shut. "Mrs. Brentwood, what's the matter?" he demanded.

"Here are the—things," she said. She fumbled with

her purse. David almost told her not to bother, then decided that he wanted verification. He took the wrinkled envelope from her hand and, opening its flap, slid out a folded form, a time-faded news clipping.

It gave him a sense of total unreality to sit inside the car, rain drumming on its roof, reading, in the greyish, wavering light, the certificate of death for *Marianna Catherine Brentwood.* Swallowing, he looked at the newspaper clipping, its headlines reading: *Local Tragedy,* its subhead: *Marianna Brentwood Dies in Accident.* As he read the brief account, he felt a strange—and even more unreal—perception that he still wasn't sure; that he had no way of knowing for certain, whether the Marianna mentioned was the one he knew. Since Thursday, he had been enveloped in a web of lies and counter lies. This could be merely an addition to them.

He shook away the feeling. It was proof; he had to believe that. Turning to Mrs. Brentwood, he said, "All right," and handed them back. "Now let's go."

With maddening deliberation, she slid the certificate and clipping back into their envelope and placed the envelope inside her purse. The click of the purse's catch made David twitch. "Well?" he said.

She turned to him, drawing in a quavering breath and forcing to her face the look of assurance which she usually displayed. "Well, what, Mister Cooper?" she replied.

His mouth fell open in astonishment and, for several moments, he couldn't speak. Finally, he snapped, "Well, *what*? Aren't you going to the house with me?"

She didn't answer.

"Obviously, you've made a study of—ghosts," he said; he still had trouble speaking the word. "You must know how they can be put to rest. Isn't there some kind of—ritual? Some way to . . . ?"

His voice trailed off, her look of detachment cowing him. "Well, isn't there?" he asked.

Mrs. Brentwood turned away. "There is not."

It was as though invisible hands had clamped around his skull and were squeezing it. David gaped at her. "There isn't?"

"No."

"But there must be!"

"I know of no such ritual," she said. "Now if you'll please get out."

David felt as if the car were turning on its side. "Mrs. Brentwood, you've spent the last few days warning me about Marianna. Are you going to tell me now that—?"

"You didn't take those warnings, Mister Cooper," she interrupted. "Now it's too late."

"Too late?" He felt completely numb, unreal again. "You're telling me that—?"

"I am telling you that there is nothing I can do."

Without warning, fury burst inside him. "Well, I don't believe it!"

Mrs. Brentwood closed her eyes. "I have told you that—"

"And I'm telling you that I don't believe it! You knew enough to answer every argument I gave before! What's happened to all that knowledge now? Has it vanished?" He cut her off. "I think you know exactly how to get rid of her!"

"If I knew how to get rid of her, don't you think I would have done it years ago?"

David gazed at her, a prickling of awareness in him.

"I don't know," he said. He peered into her eyes. "I'm not so sure."

She shuddered. "That is your prerogative," she answered stiffly. "Now if you'll get out of this car."

"You do know," he said. "You know but you won't do it."

"Mister—!"

"You know but you won't do it."

"Get out of this car, Mister Cooper!"

"Isn't that right?" he broke in. "You know but you won't do anything about it!"

"All right!" she erupted, her face a mask of sudden rage. "I *do* know how to get rid of her but I *won't*! You're right! *I will not do it!*"

"Why?!"

She pressed together shaking lips and glared at him.

"*Why?!*" he shouted.

"*Because I will not give her peace!*" she shouted back.

David jolted, stunned by the malice in her voice. "I will not give her peace," she said again. "Why should I? Did she ever give me peace? In all this world, I wanted only one thing—Terry Lawrence. I was engaged to marry him. I worshipped him.

"But Marianna wanted him; desired him, that is. Not enough for her she could have any man she chose. She had to steal my fiancé as well. She had to take Terry away from me, debauch him and destroy him. Yes! Destroy him! He was horrified of water, couldn't swim a stroke. And yet, to please her, he took up sailing. God in heaven, sailing! I warned him not to do it,

begged him. But no. He was her inamorata, her devoted slave; he did what she asked.

"And so she took him out one time too often; there
was a squall, the sailboat overturned and he was lost.
Not her, of course. Oh, no. She was an accomplished
swimmer. She reached the shore without any trouble.
Did she try to save him? She did not. She let him
drown. What did he mean to her anyway? A body to
play with, that was all. And there were lots of other
bodies to be had."

Her smile made David shiver.

"Give her peace?" she said. "I'll tell you what I'll give
her. What I've given her for more than forty years.
Justice. There's no owner in the city, Mr. Cooper; *I* own
that cottage—and whenever men come there I let them
stay a few days, let her think she's going to have her
way with them. Then I warn them off and ruin her
plans, deprive her of the one thing she exists for. Justice, Mister Cooper. Well-earned punishment. And I'll
do nothing to end it. *Nothing.*"

"Then it wasn't me," he murmured, shaken. "You
weren't concerned about saving me. You were only
interested in making sure that Marianna was alone."

"That is quite correct," she announced. "Keeping
her alone is all that *I* exist for."

"And the man who went insane?"

She set her mouth obdurately. "He chose his way,"
she said. "As you chose yours."

"*My wife didn't choose it,* Mrs. Brentwood. Will you
punish her as well?"

Her assurance seemed to waver but she forced it
back. "Marianna will doubtless leave her when the
novelty of having a body again is outweighed by its
limitations."

"And when may I expect that, Mrs. Brentwood?"

"I have no idea," she said.

"A day? A week?"

"I said—"

"A month? A year? Ten years? *Twenty*?"

"Perhaps!" she flared.

He felt his muscles quivering with repressed fury. "And in the meantime, Mrs. Brentwood?"

She made no reply and David looked at her contemptuously. "Why does any human being want to protect another?" he quoted her. He shook his head, revulsed. "How stupid you must have thought me," he said. Shoving open the door, he got out quickly.

Anger failed him as he slid behind the wheel of the car. Sick with fear, he watched the Bentley turned and driven toward the bluff. All his strength seemed drained away. "My God." He clutched a trembling hand across his eyes. "Oh, my God, my God."

What was he to do?

He listened at the door for several minutes before unlocking it quickly and entering the room.

She was on the bed again, now completely nude and lying on her back, her face heavily, almost grotesquely made up. She'd removed the wall mirror from above the bureau and set it at the foot of the bed, leaning it against the baseboard. Intent on her reflection, she didn't even glance around. Removing the key, David shut the door and re-locked it. He crossed the room, dropping the key into his trouser pocket.

As he stood beside the bed, looking down at her, her pose and actions grew increasingly lascivious. He felt nothing but despair. It wasn't Ellen doing these things. Still, unless he, somehow, managed to coerce Marianna into identifying herself, he couldn't be completely sure. He withstood a fluttering rise of panic. If it *was* Marianna (and he had to believe that) she was limited to Ellen's mind and body now, her scope, as an opponent, considerably reduced.

He steeled himself to begin. One step at a time, he thought; first: identification.

"Marianna?"

She continued eyeing her reflection, running both hands over her body in slow, lingering caresses. David felt himself bristle. He wouldn't call her Ellen. That was, clearly, what she wanted.

"You may as well look up," he said.

Her gaze shifted. "All right, I'm looking." The corners of her mouth twitched as she restrained a smile. "So are you."

Through sex, the thought came. David tightened, fearing momentarily that she could tell what he was thinking. She couldn't though; not now. He effected a smile. "Why shouldn't I look?" he asked.

Her returned smile made him feel a fragment of advantage. "That's right," she said. "Why shouldn't you? I'm your wife."

He let it pass unchallenged. She was toying with him, that was obvious. He mustn't let it make him lose his temper anymore. She was a twenty-three year old woman now and he could deal with that if he kept his mind to it. He was grateful that she'd put on so much make-up. It altered her appearance enough to be a constant reminder that she wasn't Ellen.

He tried to look intrigued as he watched what she was doing to herself with the middle finger of her right hand. "Like?" she asked.

"Uh-huh." He felt his stomach muscles throbbing. Easy.

"You want to do it?"

He drew in skittish breath. "Maybe."

"Take your clothes off then."

He had to swallow and she mocked him. "Nervous? With your own wife?"

If you were my wife, you'd go home to your daughter! The accusation lashed across his mind. He forced back the anger but knew that she'd seen his change of expression. "Oh," she chided. "Mad?"

"No."

"Well, make up your mind, lover," she said. "Or give me the keys so I can find somebody else to play with."

David shivered. "How about the studio?" he asked.

"The studio?"

"We'll do it there," he said. A wave of hopeless apprehension swept across him. What good would that do? he thought as he watched her sit up, smiling. "If you insist," she said. The smile disappeared. "You'd better make it good though." She dropped her legs across the side of the bed and stood. He put his arms around her as she pushed against him. Immediately, her breathing quickened and she started nibbling moistly at his ear lobe. "Sure you want to wait?" she murmured.

"Nicer in the studio." He had to strain to keep his voice from trembling.

"Why?" she teased.

"I'll tell you when we get there."

"Tell me now." She rubbed against him. "Show me."

He felt powerless again. Abruptly, he pulled away and moved to the bedside table. Pulling out its drawer, he took out the box of incense. "We'll burn this," he said, trying to sound interested. He looked at her with sudden curiosity, wondering what she'd say.

She asked, "What's that?"

You know what it is! he wanted to shout. He twitched, repressing the desire. "Don't you remember?"

She took the box from his hand. *"Amour Exotica,"* she read.

"Shall we burn it?"

She shrugged. "Why not?"

He looked around, trying not to show his disappointment. "Wonder where it is," he said.

"What?"

"The burner."

"Oh."

If he could trap her into finding it, prove that she knew where it was ... He turned to face her. "Maybe we can find it," he suggested.

Her smile insinuated that she knew he was playing a game of cat-and-mouse with her. David tightened, then restrained his temper. Maybe she didn't know; he mustn't defeat himself. "Let's look," he said.

He watched her from the corners of his eyes as he moved around the room, trying to convince himself that what he was doing had significance. He tightened as she raised the right-hand window seat and looked inside. "Nothing here," she said. She sounded bored and he winced, realizing that he was going to have to arouse her all over. The problem seemed insuperable and he felt like giving up. He resisted the urge and crossed to the other window seat. As he lifted it, a weight of new defeat pressed down at him. The incense burner was inside. Grimacing, he reached down and lifted it out. "Oh, good, you found it," she said.

He nodded curtly. "Let's go down now."

"Do you really want to?" she asked. Her tone intimated that at the moment, she didn't care one way or the other.

Through sex, he thought determinedly; when the body was aroused, the mind was vulnerable. I should know, he thought bitterly as he moved to her and took her in his arms. "I'm sure," he said.

He kissed her on the mouth, rubbing harsh caresses over her body. Suddenly a new fear pressed at him. What if his own mind became vulnerable? He struggled to check the responses of his flesh. Pressing his cheek to hers, he held her tightly, pretending, for a moment, that it was really Ellen, that he held her in his arms with love.

"You're hurting me," she snapped.

He let go, stared at her. God, I can't, he thought.

"I don't think you want to do anything," she said disgustedly. "Give me the goddam keys and I'll get a man myself."

He stiffened. "It'll have to be me or no one," he answered. "I won't let you out."

For an instant, he was sure that she was going to lunge at him and, flinching, he prepared himself for her attack.

It never came. Instead, surprisingly, she looked at him with pouting irritation. "Do something then," she said.

Relieved, he put an arm around her shoulders and led her toward the door. "Come on," he said.

She didn't answer. Impasse, he thought, stricken. If

he let himself become aroused enough to animate her, he might lose control and accomplish nothing. If he held himself in check, there might be no response from her at all. Again, he fought away despair. He couldn't give up now. For a moment, he considered looking for a priest; but he wasn't sure if it would help and he didn't dare think of leaving her alone for any length of time. Even less would he dare take her with him for fear that she might get away from him and be lost forever. He had no choice but to do what he was doing: groping his way along, hoping for some unknown opportunity to present itself.

"You feel cold," he said.

"I'm not."

"Wouldn't you like a robe or something?"

In that light, the scowl she gave him coupled with her garishly made-up face almost terrified him. She looked artificial—like some ghastly effigy of life. Averting his eyes, he moved ahead to the door and unlocked it, trying, in those moments, to regain his courage. He had to go on for Ellen's sake; there was no other way.

"You've forgotten how to put on make-up," he said, turning back.

"Which means—?"

"Nothing."

Her lips pursed with doubt giving her the appearance of a resentful mannequin. "If you don't like it," she said, "there's plenty of others who will."

For the first time since he'd run upstairs to find her on the bed, he sensed an air of defensiveness about her anger. He didn't know exactly what it meant but it quickened him and he filed the observation for possible later use. "Don't be so sensitive," he told her. He put an arm across her shoulders, leading her into the hall. As they moved for the stairs, he reached down and squeezed her breast, gratified at the immediate reaction, her eyes hooding, her lips tensing back. "Nice?" he asked.

"I don't want to wait," she muttered.

"Nicer in the studio," he said.

"You—" she glared at him "—bastard."

He tried not to show the increasing sense of hope he felt. He smiled and kissed her cheek. "What a thing to call the man who's going to make love to you," he said.

"It isn't love I want."

"No." He swallowed. "It's not."

"And it's not what you want either."

"Oh?" They started down the stairs. "What do I want?"

"To grovel," she said.

"Oh. Yes." He closed his fingers over her breast again, making her gasp. Suddenly, she turned and slid her arms around him, jamming her lips to his. He had to clutch at the bannister rail to keep from falling as she ground herself against him.

"Here," she whispered, "on the stairs."

He set his mind against her will. "The studio," he said.

Jerking free, she grabbed his arm and almost pulled him down the steps to the studio landing. She shoved open the door and tugged him inside.

It was like entering the interior of a beaten tympani, he thought. All around him, rain was pounding on the roof and windows, so loudly that it drowned out the crashing of the waves. He shivered. The air was frigid. "Aren't you going to be cold?" he asked.

"No." She drew him toward the couch. David wondered, with sudden fear, if she really was conjoint with Ellen's flesh. What if she felt no discomfort from the cold, allowing Ellen's body to become ill? He tried not to think about it as she led him across the room. Unexpectedly, a vision of Linda crossed his mind. She may die, he thought. He fought it off. One step at a time! It was all he could do.

"I'll open the drapes," she said and, letting go, pulled one of them aside, admitting the grey illumination of the day which, filtered through rain-shrouded glass, textured the walls and floor with a jellylike pattern of light and shadow. She turned to him and grabbed his arm again, pulling him to the couch and sitting.

David drew his hand away and held up the incense burner. "You're forgetting this," he said.

"To hell with that!" She tried to slap it from his hand but he jerked it back. "I'm warning you," she said. "I want it and I want it now." The malignance in her voice chilled him but he managed not to show it.

"Have to do it right," he said. "I thought you liked incense."

She didn't answer and he felt the sullen fury of her behind him as he set the burner on the floor, removed its top and put in one of the shriveled cakes. Removing the book of matches from his pocket, he ignited it and held it to the incense. As the first fumes reached his nostrils, he almost gagged. It was the same thick, musky odor he'd been conscious of when he'd been with Marianna.

He turned abruptly. In the wavering light, she looked, to him, like some monstrous, over-sized doll. "I have to tell you something—Ellen," he began.

Her eyes narrowed.

"I've been having an affair," he said. "With this Marianna I've been mentioning. We did it on that couch."

She stared at him, visibly confused.

"Nothing to say?" he asked. "You don't mind? It doesn't bother you that I've committed adultery right where you're sitting?"

"Why should—?"

"Does it bother you?"

"No!" she flared. "Why should it?"

"I can see her again and you won't mind?" She grimaced, looking up at him in baffled silence. "You don't mind?" he cried.

"No!"

He shuddered. "No, of course you don't. Because you're not my wife."

Her face contorted. "You dirty—!"

David pushed her back as she tried to stand. "You gave yourself away," he said, trying hard to sound amused and confident. "I hope you're not so stupid that you're still going to pretend you're my wife."

Appalled, he watched the look of rage melting from her face. At last, she smiled. "But I am," she said, "your loving wife."

David stared at her, feeling dazed and nullified. He'd accomplished nothing. So long as she continued claiming she was Ellen, he could never be positive that she wasn't. The realization shook him.

"Is that what you took me down here for?" she asked. "To convince me that I'm not your wife?" She made a scoffing noise. "You *are* an idiot."

He mustn't stop. Desperate, David sat beside her, took her hand. She snatched it away. "Listen," he said.

"I don't have to listen to you," she said. She tried to stand but he grabbed her wrist.

"You aren't going anywhere!" He held her rigidly. "You may as well listen because you aren't going to leave this house."

Her smile was thin, contemptuous. "What are you going to do?" she asked. "Chain me to the wall?"

"You won't get out."

"You're going to break—my wrist if you don't loosen up," she said. He had the distinct impression that she'd been about to say: *her* wrist. He let his grip slacken but continued holding her. "Listen to me then," he said.

"Listening." She yawned, looking toward the window.

"I know you're Marianna."

"Mm-hmm."

"I know you're thrilled to possess a body again, to feel it and—see it." He reached out with his free hand and turned her head so she'd look at him. "Listen," he said.

"Yes, yes, yes."

"It *is* a marvelous thing to have a body. But it's more marvelous to have a mind, a soul. That you still possess. But you endanger it more with every minute you stay in this house—and in my wife."

He held up her arm. "This isn't yours," he said. "It's not your body; you know that. It belongs to someone else. You're dead, Marianna. You can lie about it all you want but you know you're not alive, that you mock yourself insisting that you are. For the sake of your soul, release my wife and release your hold on this world. You don't belong here anymore."

"Shut up," she said. "Shut up. Shut up. Shut up!"

"I'm telling you the truth, Mar—"

"*Shut-up!*"

David trembled with repressed excitement. He'd gotten through to her. "Will you leave her be?" he asked. "Do that much anyway. You can't remain in her indefinitely."

Despite her fury, she was able to smile. "I think you've lost your mind," she said. "How can you talk to me like that? Your own wife."

He stiffened with wrath. "All right," he said. "If that's the way you want it." He clamped his fingers on her wrist again. "Then listen to this. I know what you want. To you, this body is nothing but an instrument for sex. Well, I've got news for you, Marianna—"

"Ellen."

"Marianna!" he shouted. "You'll never get a chance to use this body. I'll watch you every second—keep you tied up all day, drugged all night so I can sleep. You'll never have another man as long as you stay in this body. You understand me, Marianna? Never! You won't even get a chance to touch it!"

Her expression told him that he'd frightened her and, before she could recover, he went on, "You'd better leave her, Marianna, leave her now. If you don't, I promise you a nightmare. Before, you had this house, at least. You could move around in it and wait. Maybe a man would come, maybe you could control him. Not now, Marianna. Not now. You had only your sister to contend with then. Now you have me. I'm out of your reach but you're not out of mine. This isn't a body you've entered, Marianna, it's a prison. And I'm your guard. You're in solitary confinement and there you'll stay, I promise you. Look forward to an endless agony, Marianna. An endless agony and nothing more—"

He broke off, gasping, as her head dropped forward. She began to fall and he caught her startledly, his heartbeat jarring. "What—?" He stared at her in shock, not knowing what to do; he twitched as she slumped against him. With trembling fingers, he lifted her chin and looked at her. Her eyes were shut, her mouth hung open slackly. With a frightened whimper, David pushed two fingers underneath her left breast, relieved yet newly baffled by the steady pulsing of her heart.

Shuddering, he lay her back and pushed to his feet. With nervous haste, he lifted her legs and swung them around to the couch, bending over to shift her limp weight until she was stretched out. Grabbing the blanket, he spread it across her, tucking it around her sides.

He was just sitting down to chafe her wrists when she opened her eyes. She sobbed and, twisting over, pressed against him, clinging to his legs. "David."

He stared at her, dumbstruck. Gingerly, he ran a shaking hand across her cheek. "Ellen?"

"Yes."

"Oh—!" He pulled her violently against himself, a groan of relief in his throat. "El . . . darling."

"David . . ."

He kissed her cheeks, her lips, her throat. "Thank God; thank God."

"What happened? Did I fall asleep?"

He hesitated. "Yes," he said, "you did. Well, more than that but I'll tell you about it later. Right now, let's get out of here."

She blinked. "I feel so weak."

"No wonder."

"What happened?"

"Oh—" He smiled infirmly. "It's a long story, El; a *long* story." He brushed the back of a hand across his wet cheeks. "I'll tell you on the plane."

"Hold me, David."

"Yes." He wrapped his arms around her, clasping her tightly as if to protect her from all danger. "God, I'm glad you're back, El, I'm so glad you're back."

"Back?" she asked.

The sound he made was partly laughter, partly a groan of dismay at the prospect of explaining what had happened. "I'll just have to tell you later, sweetheart. I haven't got the strength right now, I really haven't."

"All right." She rubbed her hands across his back. "All right, darling." She shivered. "I'm *cold*," she said.

"I know."

She looked around, perplexed. "Why are we in here?" she asked.

"Part of the story, El. Such a story; you may never believe it."

She shivered again. "So cold," she murmured. She felt beneath the blanket. "I have nothing on," she said, confusedly.

"Come on, we'll get you dressed."

She started up, fell back again. "I can't," she said, "I feel so weak." Her teeth began to chatter. "And cold." She looked at him pleadingly. "Lie beside me, David? Please?"

"Yes, darling." Hastily, he lay beside her, pulling the blanket across them both. She pushed against him with a groan, sliding both her arms around his body. David winced. "You *are* cold."

Shivering, she rubbed against him and he turned to face her. She slid her right leg over his left and pressed against him as hard as she could. "You're so warm," she said.

"Oh, El." He hugged her fiercely, eyes closed, his cheek pressed to hers. Thank God," he thought. The nightmare was ended. They could go home now, see Mark and—

David caught his breath, remembering. Opening his eyes, he said, "We better—"

He stopped. She was smiling at him.

"Ellen?"

"What, darling?"

"We'd better be on our way."

"Of course." She kissed him gently. "Darling?"

"What?"

"Before we go—"

"Yes?"

"Would you . . . make—love to me?"

Something in the way she spoke the words made David freeze. He stared into her eyes, a crawling sensation on his scalp.

"What is it, darling?"

He couldn't speak.

"Don't you want to?"

"Make—love?" he asked.

"Please."

Like a gush of icy water, fury shot up from the depths of him. He jerked away, his face gone rigid, pale.

"What is it, David?"

"Never mind the masquerade." His voice was low and trembling.

"Masquerade?"

He jarred to his feet, glaring at her. "You miserable bitch," he said.

"I don't under—"

"Stop it! Marianna."

"What?" She gaped at him.

"It's over! Drop it! I know who you are!"

"David, what's the matter with you?"

"I'm a gullible idiot, that's what's the matter with me," he snapped. He felt like hitting her. "I should have known you wouldn't give up that easily." He leaned over her, scowling. "And you should have known that you aren't clever enough to carry it off."

"David—"

"Stop it!—damn you. I'm not buying it anymore, don't you understand? You went too far. You always will. Do you really think my wife would talk of making love when our daughter may be dying in a hospital!" He grimaced with loathing. "Making love," he said. "You couldn't even say the *words* convincingly."

She made no attempt to answer him now.

"You and your great love for Terry Lawrence," he continued, scornfully. "All you love is flesh." He sat beside her, grabbed her wrist again. "Well, nothing's changed," he said. "Nothing at all. I'm going to take you home and keep you locked up day and night."

She tightened. "Oh?"

"Yes; Oh. *Oh*, Marianna. You haven't got a chance."

"Maybe I'll manage," she said.

"Will you, Marianna?"

"I'm Ellen, darling; I'm your wife." She smiled. "Why don't you tie me to the couch now?"

"You think you're going to get away from me eventually, don't you?"

She didn't answer and he nodded. "Well, perhaps you would," he said. "Perhaps I'd better make a different plan."

Her smile was gone. She looked at him suspiciously.

"Perhaps I'd better have you committed," he said.

She started to speak but he cut her off. "Believe me, it's possible," he said. "A lot of people in Los Angeles know my wife, know the way she behaves." He shook his head as if pitying her. "You couldn't convince them in a hundred years. When they see how *you* behave, they'll be lining up for blocks to commit you."

He clamped his hand on her wrist. "Do you know what it is to be committed, Marianna? Let me tell you. It won't be only me watching you. I'd make a mistake, sooner or later. I'd overlook something, fall asleep, blunder somehow and you'd get away. But you won't get away from them, Marianna. In an institution, there'll be an entire staff of people to keep you under lock and key. I'll tell them you're violent, suicidal. They'll put you in a straitjacket and keep you locked in a little room with bars on the window. There'll be no men. I'll tell them you're a sexual psychopath. You'll never have a man again." He leaned in close. "All you'll have is shock treatments. Baths in icy water. Constant supervision and confinement. Oh, you won't like it, Marianna. You won't like it at all.

"On the other hand," he said, "if you'll leave my wife, I'll take her home and you can have this house again. I'm not concerned about your soul now; I don't give a damn about your soul. As far as I'm concerned, you can stay here forever. Your sister isn't going to live much longer. When she's gone, there'll be no interference at all, you can do whatever you please."

He paused. "Make up your mind," he said, then. "I'm losing patience. Take your choice: this house and your freedom—or being locked up for good."

She shuddered violently. I'm winning! David thought. "Make up your mind!" he ordered.

Her smile was such a shock to him that his face went blank before he could prevent it.

"Well," she said. She shrugged. "If that's what you

want to do with me, I can't stop you. If you want to have your wife put in a straitjacket and locked in a room with bars on the window, I can't prevent it."

"Marianna—"

"I'm not Marianna, darling. You've made a mistake. I'm Ellen; your wife." Her look of distress bordered on satire. "And you're going to lock me up," she said. "You're going to put me away for good."

He knew that he was trembling but he couldn't stop. She'd beaten him again. She knew full well that he could never put Ellen in an institution, that the threat had been a pointless one. Dear God, there's no way out, he thought in anguish.

"What's the matter, darling?"

"All right," he said. "I won't commit you."

"Oh." She looked at him with mocking sympathy. "And it was such a good idea."

"I already had a good idea."

"Oh, yes. You're going to keep me tied up—no, locked up, isn't it? That's right. You're going to keep me in a closet all day and drugged all night. Except, of course, as you said, you'll blunder. You'll make a mistake; overlook something. Then I'll be gone. Driving into Port Jefferson, maybe even New York."

"Oh?"

"Yes; oh. *Oh*, David. I'll go to a bar and pick up a man, maybe two men. I'd like that; two at once." She flicked her tongue at him. "That's what you've taught me, you see. Your Ellen's not a prude anymore. She's going to taste the wine of life. To the dregs—David, little David."

"Port Jefferson," he said. "New York."

"Go on, tie me to the couch," she told him. "Lock me in a closet. Drug me."

Port Jefferson; New York, he thought. Something there. "I intend to," he said. He studied her face and, suddenly, it came to him. *"But not here,"* he finished. Jarring to his feet, he hauled her up and started pulling her toward the door.

"What do you think you're doing?" Caught off-guard, her voice betrayed sudden alarm. He was right! She started holding back. "What are you doing?"

"Taking you home, what else?"

She stiffened. "What?"

"It's simple; don't you understand?" He heard her bare feet squeaking on the floor boards as she tried to brake herself. "I'm taking you home."

"You're not taking me any—!"

"But I am!" he cut her off. "Right out of this house!"

She swung too suddenly for him to avert the blow; he staggered as her flattened hand smashed against his cheek. He almost lost his grip, the studio wheeling around him, darkness gushing at the fringes of his sight. He heard her shout, "Let go of me!" and, reacting blindly, swung at her. She lurched back, gasping, as he slapped her face.

"You *can't* go, can you?!" he cried. "You're afraid to leave!"

She tried to hit him again. This time, he blocked it with his left arm, wincing as their wrists collided; she hissed and dropped her hand. Even as her face was twisted by the pain, he slapped her a second time. With a cry of shock, she floundered aside. David yanked her back so sharply that her head snapped. He began to drag her toward the hall again. "Let's see how tough you are when you're a hundred miles from here," he said. "A thousand; three thousand!"

She flung herself against him, face distorted by

pain-wrenched fury. It was a maniac who fought him—scratching, kicking, biting, shrieking at him with demented hate. David struggled with her doggedly. Achieving a grip at last, he twisted her right arm behind her back until she froze. "You're Marianna, aren't you?" he said.

"Let go."

"You're Marianna, aren't you?"

"God damn you!"

"Aren't you?" He twisted harder; it was Ellen's arm but it had to be done. She screamed. "Let go of me, you bastard!"

"Aren't you?!"

She clenched her teeth and started whining hideously.

"All right." He shoved her toward the door. "I'll take you home then."

She recoiled berserkly, the whine increasing in volume until it flooded from her lips in a piercing scream. David set his mind against the terrifying sound and kept on pushing. They were almost to the door now.

"No!" she shrieked. "Don't take me out of here!"

"You're Marianna, aren't you?!"

"Don't take me out of here!"

"You're Marianna, aren't you?!"

"Yes! Yes! Yes!" She started crying wretchedly and David stopped. Thank God, he thought.

"Please let go of me," she begged.

He loosened his grip but did not release her. "Let go of my wife then."

"I can't."

He twisted her arm again. "You can."

She shook her head, groaning.

"Get out of her or I swear I'll take you away."

"Stay here," she pleaded, "I'll do anything you say."

"Let go of my wife!"

"I can't!" The words erupted into a scream of agony as he twisted her arm.

"Damn you, let her go!" he raged.

Her sudden, reactive blow caught him by surprise, her left elbow battering into his cheek with concussive force. David cried out and staggered to his right, clutching at his face. Pain shot through his cheek and eye in jagged, fiery lines.

"I won't!" she raged. "You'll never make me! I'm too strong for you! I can do anything I want! I made you go after your wife that morning, then made you stop so I could use your body for myself! Every time you tried to take her, I kept you from it! I control you! You can't do anything I don't want you to do! Do you want to know why I said goodbye to you so cheerfully? Because I knew you'd never leave! I put your wife to sleep and had you again! I can do anything I want!—*anything*!"

"Not now you can't," he answered shakily, still half blinded by the pain. "You're in that body and it's all you have; and now I know your secret. You're afraid to leave the area you knew in life. But I can make you leave." He started toward her groggily.

She backed off, glaring at him. "Get away from me."

"Get out of her," he said.

"All right!" A frightening smile twisted back her lips. "I'll get out. But if I can't have the body, you won't either!" Whirling, she rushed toward the windows.

David stumbled after her, then held back. Trembling fitfully, he watched her turn at the window and laugh at him. "All right!" she said. She fisted her hands as though to drive them through the glass. He couldn't breathe, his heartbeats so gigantic that his body jolted. He forced himself to stand immobile.

She looked confused. Obviously, she expected him to chase her.

"Well?" he asked. "What are you waiting for?"

Her mouth slipped open and, despite the pain and dread, he knew that he had gambled right again. She wanted Ellen's body too much to destroy it.

"All right!" she cried. She turned and raised her hands. David stiffened, leaning forward. After a while, he leaned back, releasing steamlike breath. "You can't," he said.

The sob that broke in her was as pitiable as it was appalling. "Oh, God," she moaned. "Oh, God, oh, God. To live again. To be in flesh. Nobody knows—the agony; the pain! Bodiless! Useless! God!" she screamed. "I want my body! *Take my soul but give me back my body!*"

Groaning dementedly, she sank to her knees, clutching at the window sill. He had never heard such a sound in his life. In spite of everything, he thought: God help her, she's in torment. Whatever she had done to him was nothing in comparison to what she had done to herself. How could her sister hate such a pitiful creature? Earthbound, he thought; how terrifying a description. To have eternity waiting and yet, of one's own accord, to create a prison in which the soul must lodge in everlasting desolation. Surely, this was Hell.

He walked unevenly to where she knelt and crouched beside her. "Marianna?"

She could only weep.

"Go on," he said. "Don't stay here anymore. There's nothing here but sorrow."

She shook her head.

"Yes," he said. "You've been here long enough.
Don't profane yourself any longer. Go on."

"I can't."

"Why not?"

"I can't, I can't."

"Why, Marianna?"

"I'm afraid."

"Of what?"

"The dark." She raised her face and stared upward
with a look of terror. "The *dark*," she said. "The punishment."

"How do you know—?"

"I know!" she cried. "I know what's out there! Darkness! I'm afraid of it! I won't go there alone!" She
turned to face him, cheeks glistering with tears, eyes
round with dread. "No matter what you do to me, I
won't go there alone."

He swallowed dryly. "What if you're not alone?" he
asked. He felt unreal again.

"If I'm—not alone?"

"Will you leave my wife if I go with you?" Suddenly,
it was the only answer and he knew it. She was like a
child—terrified, irrational. No amount of threatening
would avail him now. He recognized her terror. There
was only one way to dispel it; one way he could save
Ellen.

She was staring at him, an expression of uncertain
hope on her face. "You'll go with me?"

David braced himself against the waves of dizziness that pulsed across his brain. "I will," he said.

She shuddered. "Will you—hold my hand?" she
asked.

"I will." He stood up, feeling numbed and strange,

the imminence of death around him like a cloud. He wasn't frightened though; that was the strangest part of all. He felt as he had that day—inspired and transcended. He reached down and took her hand; he helped her up. "Leave her now," he said. "Come with me. I'll take care of you."

"Don't lie to me," she begged. "Please don't lie to me." She sounded so afraid, so like a terror-stricken child that David caught his breath and smiling at her, clenched his left hand and drove it through the window next to him.

The cut was deep yet he hardly felt it. Looking down, he saw blood spilling out across his palm. "Oh," he said. He shivered. "God." He closed his eyes, holding her hand tightly. Forgive me, he thought. He drew in shaking breath and clenched his teeth. The pain was starting now. Ellen; it's for you, he thought. I love you and I give you life. "For you," he whispered. He lowered his arm and, after several moments, opened his eyes. "Leave her now," he said.

His face went blank.

She was smiling at him.

"What?" he mumbled.

She glanced at his wrist.

"What?" He felt himself begin to weave.

"You're bleeding, David."

"Leave her!"

She jerked her hand away. "I've changed my mind," she said.

He began to stagger, caught himself.

"I just realized that, after you're gone, I can have the body all to myself," she said.

"Marianna—!" He stumbled toward her but she backed off, smiling. The room spun sideways and, crying out, he toppled to the floor, gasping at the pool of blood he landed in. "No!" He tried to stand but couldn't. "Marianna, please—!"

"Oh," she said with mocking sympathy. "Poor David. He's going to die." She smiled again. "And I'll be all alone with this beautiful body. My sister won't be able to chase men away from the cottage anymore. I can have all the men I want."

Something flickered across David's mind—a wavering streak of clarity. "The cottage," he said. He forced himself to stand. "The cottage . . ."

"Yes, the cottage," she said. "The wonderful, marvelous cottage."

The room swam around him as he started toward her. Still, his mind was growing clearer by the moment; as blood and life ran from his wrist, awareness kept increasing strangely. "You talk about Port Jefferson, New York," he said. "That's not the way it is at all though, is it? You can't drive to either of them. You can't even go out to the car, can you?"

A look of wary resistance tensed her face and she backed away from him. "What are you talking about?" She tried to sound contemptuous but couldn't; fear was straining at her voice.

"You're a prisoner here." The clarity was full now; there was no question in his mind. "Even in my wife's body, you can't leave the cottage." He was aware of speaking through clenched teeth, of breathing laboredly. But he knew; he knew. "You died here and no matter what you want to do, you have to stay here."

"You're a fool," she answered. But her face was pale, she kept retreating.

With a sudden, willful burst of strength, David lunged at her. She tried to jump back but her bare feet slipped on the wooden floor and she lost her balance, falling to one knee. David grabbed her right wrist with his right hand and hauled her back up. "What are you doing?" she asked. Her voice was faint.

He didn't speak but started pulling her toward the broken window. Darkness swirled up from the floor at him; he willed it off. He'd do this, then he'd die. It was the one thing he had strength to accomplish.

"What are you doing?" she demanded. She tried to hold him back but couldn't. There was a fierce strength in his will that went beyond the failing of his body. He dragged her now, his eyes intent on the window, his left wrist spattering a jagged trail of blood along the floor.

"No." She started twisting, kicking. "No!"

"Yes!" The roar of his voice made her suddenly limp. "We're leaving you behind!"

She tried to scream in protest but there was no time. Her scream became one of stark, consuming horror as he dragged her up onto the couch and, hugging her against himself, leaped backward, shattering the window and pulling both of them into the darkness and the rain, downward toward the wet sand, David holding Ellen on top of him so that, when they landed, he would die and she would live.

Seconds later, there was impact, pain and sweeping blackness.

EPILOGUE

D avid stared across the bedroom. Through the picture window, he could see the blue-green glowing of the pool, the glitter of the city lights below. How far away he felt from that cottage in Logan Beach. It seemed another world. The only tangible evidence that it existed at all was the dark red scar across his wrist.

Beyond that, it seemed the recollection of a dream—indistinct and fading. A ghost in his life? His life was here in Sherman Oaks. With Ellen who was, at the moment, showering. With Mark who was spending the night with a friend in Malibu. With Linda and Bill and his grandson, Peter David, who, this very afternoon, had been on his lap, laughing with delight. These were the rudiments of his existence, solid and precise.

He looked at his wrist. The scar would grow less apparent in time, the memory diminish. Even now, eight months later, he could not, accurately, recall that night; it had been too distorted, too bizarre. Then, too, there had been only blackness from the time he'd been knocked unconscious until he'd woken in a hospital room, his wrist stitched and bandaged, Ellen sitting by his bedside, looking at him anxiously; weeping as he smiled. The fall had been virtually harmless to her, only shaking her up; somehow she'd gotten him to an emergency hospital.

Lasting memories began at that point, the clearest of these to do with the plane ride home and with his telling Ellen about Marianna and what had happened in that period from Thursday afternoon on. The four-plus hours on the jet had been, if anything, more pain-ful than the four-plus days in Logan Beach for he had had to watch her face reflecting, one by one, each pain and sorrow she'd experienced during that time.

From that day, to this moment, something had left their relationship. What it was he wasn't sure—a spark, perhaps. In other respects, their marriage was much sounder. There were no more secrets; none that he was conscious of, at any rate. They spoke now, aired their griefs and voiced their differences, their attitudes. The marriage seemed secure. If something had gone from it, he had to accept that something as having been expendable. For he would not go back to the way things had been. Lacking a better word, the "spark" might have disappeared but, in its place, was a depth of understanding and mutual respect which had not been there before. As far as he was concerned, that was nothing but improvement.

No longer did he think in terms of *I*. He tried, con-sciously, never to feel sorry for himself—and, he had not absolved himself from his share of blame regard-ing Marianna. He *had* been responsible—not fully, perhaps but neither could he white-wash his part in it. Obviously, he would never know what percentage of his downfall had been due to Marianna's influence, what percentage due to his own, personal lack. All he did know—and he knew it definitely—was that, if it hadn't been for his particular frame of mind, what had happened might never have occurred at all. Marianna had been waiting, true; but it had been for a certain type of man that she waited most. He had been that type.

God willing, he would not permit himself to be that type again.

He turned onto his side, looking at the bathroom door. The shower had been turned off; Ellen would be coming in soon. He wondered if they'd make love tonight. That area of their relationship had, also, improved even though that certain "spark" had been extinguished there as well. The "spark," he suddenly decided, was immature romanticism. Very well, then, they were not as wildly passionate as they had been in their youth. There, still, was gentleness and patience, kindness, understanding. There, still, was wisdom and companionship.

And there was self control—the realization that physical desires had to be subordinate to the mind; a realization that had taken him a long time to accept. It had been so much simpler to allow the body to speak for itself for it was never without something to say and its commands were easy to follow. So easy, in fact, that, in time, they became an addiction.

But, to the body, there were no individuals, no personalities to be cared for. To the body there was only raw sensation. With whom that sensation occurred made no difference. The body was an animal demanding periodic food. He had satisfied that hunger, all unquestioning. Now he had to discipline the beast—which would not be simple because it had become accustomed to its license. Yet it had to be done—and, after all, it *was* only an animal. It possessed neither subtlety nor logic; it only raged and craved. If the mind could not control such a creature, then the mind might just as well not exist.

It was his aspiration, now, to permanently encage that animal within his mind. Not destroy it; not break its spirit, turning it into a vapid drudge. Its wildness was not entirely undesirable. Much of it had a fine and vital beauty. Still, he had to keep it within confines, be able to release it only when he chose. The cage must not be so flimsy that the animal could break out whenever it pleased and roam his mental countryside, an uncontrollable predator. It had to have its limits. Within these, it could have its head—but the limits had to exist.

There is the body and there is the mind, he thought. All complexities stripped away, it was as simple as that. Man's birthright was a body—but it was also a mind with which to control that body and transcend it. With his mind, man could make, of his relationship to woman, something magnificent. The joining of their minds (and of their souls, perhaps) was infinitely more important than the joining of their bodies. Their physical relationship must be, in fact, a manifestation, in flesh, of their higher relationship—an expression of their love.

Anything less was, to varying degrees, mutual and self destruction.

David turned onto his back, smiling at himself. To understand the problem was not solve it, he thought. A modicum of insight did not create the whole person, contrary to scripts the like of which, God help him, he, himself, had written. There still were years of work ahead. There would probably be backslidings. But, at least, he had a direction now and he would never turn from it again.

The bathroom door was opened and he pushed up, looking at her, at his Ellen. Her hair was longer now (to his amazed surprise, he'd only had to ask her once to let it grow), tinted slightly (as a gesture to their new relationship, she'd said) and she was wearing a long, pale-blue nightgown. She looked fresh and clean and David felt a sudden longing for her. Sitting up, he dropped his legs across the mattress edge and said, "Come here."

Ellen crossed the room and stood before him. "Yes?"

"Sit down." He patted his lap.

"All right." She settled on his legs and David put his arms around her, nuzzling his face against her neck. "Smells good," he murmured.

"Does it?"

"Mmm." He began to kiss her neck, casually at first, then with increasing ardor. Ellen stroked his hair.

"I love you, El," he said.

"I love you too."

Those were only words, he thought. "I mean it, El. I'm not just talking." Eyes closed, he rubbed his face against her neck. "You have no idea how much I love you. No idea at all because I haven't really told you in a long, long time. But I do; I do. You're my joy—my happiness. You're my life, El."

"David . . ." Faint, uncertain.

"I mean it, El."

"I know you do."

"I hope so. I want you to believe me. I know it's been a long time, far too long, but now I'm saying it, so please believe me."

Something seemed to break inside him. "Oh, God, El, how I love you."

Pulling up his head, he pressed his lips to hers, tightening his arms around her. He kissed her cheeks and eyes, her forehead and temples, her ears, her neck again; he couldn't get enough of kissing her warm, fragrant skin. "I love you so," he murmured. "Ellen, Ellen."

Clearly, she was moved—and yet surprised as well, a bit confused. He didn't blame her. He had not been so demonstrative in years. And yet he couldn't help it now. There was no deliberation; it was all spontaneous, a rushing of emotion as desire and love enveloped him completely. She *was* his life. He couldn't exist without her, she was everything to him.

"El, lie beside me, please lie down beside me."

"Yes, sweetheart, yes." Standing quickly, she looked down at him. "Shall I take my nightgown off?" she asked.

"Yes; I want to feel you close to me." He lay down, watching her. She shivered as the silk slid up across her rigid-nippled breasts. She tossed the gown across the foot of the bed, switched off the closest bedside lamp, then lay beside him. David shuddered as she pressed against his body, her hands slipping beneath his arms to clutch at his back. They kissed impassionedly, a kiss of lovers newly meeting.

"Ellen."

"Yes."

"Do you love me?"

"Yes."

"Please tell me, tell me that you do." His hands cupped her cheeks and he looked into her eyes pleadingly. "Tell me that you love me, El, please tell me."

"I *do*, I *do*."

"Then *tell* me. I want to hear the words. I need them, El. Please tell me that you love me."

Ellen's eyes were glistening now; a tear ran down and touched his hand. "I love you, David. I love you. I love you. I love you."

What swept across him was as violent a feeling as he'd ever known. In an instant, his identity seemed gone and he and Ellen were a oneness which was larger than their sum. The love he made to her possessed no taint of self indulgence; what might have been carnality and egoism was now devotion. His actions were the same but, motivated, as they were, by loving care, they elevated each sensation to a height which he had never reached before, an altitude of ratified emotion which dizzied and exalted him.

And still he climbed!

What length of time it lasted he could not be sure. By the clock, it might have been no longer than a minute—but, to him, it was a full eternity. At the end of which they reached the climax of their mutual ascent together, clinging to each other, trembling, crying, moaning with an ecstasy which could not be expressed because it was of mind and body at the same time, an ecstasy so powerful that it stopped the world and time and life itself until they had experienced its beauty to the end.

Only then did sights and sounds impinge, did the earth begin its creaking turn and life commence once more. David held her closely, feeling the trickle of her breath across his shoulder. This is marriage, came the thought—a union and a bond. No spark left? He almost laughed, the notion now seemed so preposterous. God in Heaven! His mind reeled before the truth—or what inkling of the truth he'd managed to perceive.

"It was love," he murmured.

"Yes," she murmured back.

"It was love—all love."

"I know."

"We'll always love each other; always."

"Yes."

"I mean always, Ellen. Not just now or here. Forever. This is just the start. I believe it, El. I really do."

She kissed him with an infinite tenderness and answered, softly, "I believe it too."

She sat at the dressing table, applying a heavy coat of lipstick. Done, she put the lipstick down and ran her hands up through the jet black thickness of her hair. "Not bad," she said. "They'll never know." She peered at her features in the mirror. The makeup was a little excessive but they'd never know.

She pulled back the edges of the dressing gown and looked at her reflected body. "Here's the problem," she said. She lifted her sagging, white breasts, digging her fingers into their bulbous softness. "I hate them," she said. She scowled. "Why did you get so old?" she muttered.

She sighed. "Oh, well. At least they're real."

She smiled scornfully at the reflection of her face. "That was so stupid of you, Grace," she said. She shook her head. "Coming here to help them. Rushing in like that with your stupid cross and Bible." She laughed. "If you'd only waited a few seconds, I'd have been alone again and at your mercy. Now . . ."

She drew her robe shut. "It's an ugly body but it's real, Grace. Guess I'll keep it."

Standing she moved to the window and looked out at the beach. It was her favorite kind of day; overcast and cold. Maybe someone would pass the cottage soon; some man—or woman, it didn't matter. She thought about Grace's servant. He was awfully old but . . . She made a sound of casual estimation. Maybe when he brought supplies next week.

She chuckled softly, remembering the look of shock on Grace's face when she rushed into the studio to see both David and his wife gone out the window and, waiting for her, smiling, the one person she'd avoided all these years. She remembered how Grace had backed off, shaking her head, dropping the Bible and cross, a look of blind terror on her face. It had been such wonderful revenge to rush at her with a shriek of triumph.

And take her.

She turned and walked across the room. She'd make some supper now. Eating again was still fun. Maybe, later, a man would walk by and she could invite him in. And make Grace's body do more things than Grace had ever dreamed about.

"Or *did* you dream of doing them?" she said, amused. "Maybe this is what you wanted all along."

She laughed as she crossed the hallway. "It better be," she said, "because you're going to be here for a long, long time, dear sister."

Marianna's icy laughter filled the staircase as she went downstairs.